Spinebreaker
Book Two in the Library Gate Series
H. Duke

Table of Contents

Dear reader

Thank you for reading *Spinebreaker,* the second book in the Pagewalker series. You can sign up for my reader group at www.hdukeauthor.com. I regularly host giveaways and send out free stories.
When you're done reading, please leave an honest review—it really does make a difference.
Enjoy the story!
-H. Duke

Chapter One

"Are you a golf man, Thad?"

Mason's folded hands rested on the desk in front of him. Mason's home office always reminded Thad of the headmaster's office at the British primary school he boarded at. Everything was made of polished wood and Thaddeus was only there when he was in trouble.

Mason was the director of the agency's midwestern division, and Thaddeus' boss.

Did Mason put the smallest chair possible in front of his desk on purpose? He liked to employ these little shows of power. Thaddeus' knees were already cramping.

"No, sir."

"It's a wonderful game. Why, just last week—"

Mason did this every time Thaddeus met him. He'd ask about a subject, and if Thaddeus showed even the slightest amount of interest, he'd move on to the next thing until he found something Thaddeus didn't care to talk about, and then he'd talk about it at length.

Thaddeus had learned to tune out, paying only enough attention to respond with *yes sir, no sir, very good, sir,* at the right moments. This wasn't a conversation, it was a display.

"Well," Mason said after at least twenty minutes, "I suppose we should get to the matter at hand."

Thaddeus snapped out of his stupor. "Yes, sir."

Mason opened the report that Thaddeus had submitted the week before. "Your failure last week was unfortunate. What the heck happened? In your initial report you indicated that the Pagewalker agreed to our terms."

"She did," Thaddeus said. "She renounced her status."

"So what went wrong?"

"She changed her mind."

"You mean you allowed her to change her mind."

"Sir, I don't see how I have any control over—"

Mason raised his voice. "The building wasn't secured. She and her group were able to infiltrate it."

"We apprehended them—"

"At which point they were inadequately supervised and allowed to escape." Mason folded his hands and considered Thaddeus gravely. "You held the portal *in your grasp*. The fact that you lost it is a testament to your incompetence. What would your father think?"

Thaddeus winced at the mention of his father. He'd been working on decommissioning the last portal since before Thaddeus was born, and it wasn't until shortly before his death that Thaddeus inherited it. His father had considered it his life's greatest failure. He'd made Thaddeus promise that he would succeed where he'd failed. Thaddeus had ruined his opportunity to make good on that promise.

Mason continued. "If you weren't your father's son, I would remove you from this project immediately."

Thaddeus' head snapped up. He hadn't let himself to hope that he'd be allowed to stay on the portal case. "Sir?"

"You need to redeem yourself, of course."

"Anything. What do you want me to do?"

"Simple. I want you to offer the Pagewalker a job."

What? He couldn't be serious. "A job? Sir, I don't think—"

"With two civillians and a dog, she outsmarted your entire team. Now, doesn't that sound like someone we want on our payroll?"

Thaddeus shook his head. "She won't agree."

"Oh, I think she may have cause to join us, considering recent events." Mason opened his laptop and turned it around. A video was paused, showing the front entrance of the library.

"What is this?" Thaddeus asked. "The library doesn't have security cameras."

"This is footage from an apartment complex adjacent to the library—our techs were able to magnify it and clean up the resolution. It was taken the night after the incident. This is around nine fifteen." Mason hit play. The doors opened and the Pagewalker and one of the men from that night, the *character,* Dorian Gray, stepped out.

"Where are they going?"

"Security footage from an ATM shows them walking into a bar a few blocks away. Now, if we jump ahead..." he clicked another button, and the image on the screen changed. In this frame, a man dressed in a white polo and black pants walked up to the door and unlocked it.

"The library security guard," Thaddeus said. "What's he doing there?"

"Just watch." The next clip Mason played was from well past midnight. April and the character had returned to the library. They were now accompanied by the black man and his dog. Thaddeus now knew the man's name was Randall Washington. They stumbled up the stone steps and entered the library.

Mason forwarded through fifteen minutes of screen time, then hit play. The library doors burst open, and the Pagewalker stumbled out. Her hands were pressed over her mouth. She leaned over the railing and vomited. Washington came out of the doors behind her. They spoke for a few moments, then he led her out of view of the camera.

"What happened?"

"Just keep watching." Mason increased the playback speed again. They watched until the sky began to lighten. No one else entered that door until staff arrived the following morning.

"The security guard never came out," Thaddeus said.

"Bingo." Mason said with a smile. "We've watched days of footage, and footage of the other entrances. He never left the building. We thought this was suspicious, so we sent agents to investigate during open hours. According to the daytime staff, he hasn't reported to work since the previous night. They believe he skipped town."

"So either he slipped out unseen—"

"Highly unlikely. We have footage from other entrances, as well." Mason interjected.

"—he entered a world, or he died."

"If he entered a world, a character would have to come out in his place before five in the morning, otherwise—" he spread his fingers wide to imitate an explosion. "We've cross-referenced all the videos. Every person who has come out of that library entered it. No one is unaccounted for except the security guard."

Thaddeus sat back in his chair. "So you think his death will motivate her to join us?"

"It will have opened her eyes to the portal's destructive nature. She was distraught in that video. She looks motivated enough to me. Or at least, *motivatable*. It's your job to motivate her."

"How can you be so sure that the gate was involved in his death? You have no proof."

"Whatever happened, the portal was involved. If a bookshelf fell on him or he hanged himself, they wouldn't have bothered to cover it up."

"What if she turns down the offer?"

Mason's eyes grew dark. "Then we will have to escalate our tactics. But I trust you won't let me down."

"Yes, sir."

Chapter Two

Knock knock. "Sweetheart, someone is here to see you," Gram's voice penetrated through the wood of her bedroom door.

April closed her eyes. Who would be coming here to see her? She hadn't heard from any of her friends in months. They'd slowly disappeared after Gram got sick.

"April? It's Randall."

April's eyes shot open. Randall? What was he doing here? Outside of her door, Gram said how nice it was for the library to send someone to visit sick employees. She cooed over Rex, saying how modern it was that the library allowed pets at work.

April sighed. "Come in."

The door opened. Randall's large frame filled the door. "I'll go make some tea," Gram said.

"That would be lovely, ma'am," Randall said. "We just wanted to check in on April and make sure she's okay."

"That flu going around is a doozy," Gram said. "Luckily the doctor said my immune system is still healthy enough that I can look after her."

April swallowed. She should be looking after Gram, not the other way around.

Randall paused as he entered the room, and April could feel his gaze linger on the piles of clothes and blankets scattered across the floor. Thank God Gram had insisted on taking out the half-eaten bowls of soup.

He sat in the rocking chair next to her bed. Rex lay down on the floor with a yawn.

"Did Dorian send you?" April asked, not looking at him. "He's called a couple times."

Randall shook his head. "I haven't seen him since we found Andre." he trailed off, and April knew what he was thinking. She closed her eyes, trying to block out the memory of walking back into the Werner Room, slightly tipsy from one too many beers at the pub, and finding Andre's body on the floor, a bloom of bright red on his otherwise clean white work polo. It had spread out on the floor, like spilled Kool-aid...

She pressed the base of her thumbs into her eye sockets hard enough to produce painful bursts of stars. She felt warm, furry pressure on her lap and when she opened her eyes she found that Rex had jumped up on the bed and was lying on her.

"Hey," Randall said. "Are you okay?"

"Why did Andre come back?" April said. "He wasn't supposed to be there."

Randall shook his head. "We don't know," he said. "We probably won't ever know. That doesn't change the fact that it wasn't your fault."

"If I'd just let Thaddeus take the gate..."

"You didn't know what was going to happen. You did it to protect all those people in the books. To protect Dorian."

April blinked. She hated herself for it, but if she could go back and change her decision, trade the safety for all the people in the books for Andre, she'd do it in a hearbeat.

"I just wish I could take it back," she said. She kept thinking about that night. Whenever she managed to sleep, she had dreams about being in that moment, turning down Dorian's proposition to go to the bar... but no matter what, Andre always walked in and got shot.

Randall sat down on the edge of the bed next to Rex. He placed his hand on the dog's head and was quiet for close to a minute.

"I was on the front lines in Iraq," Randall said. "One night, I was patrolling the perimeter with one of the guys. His name was Brad. This local boy comes up to us asking for a drink of water in broken English. Kid was ten, maybe eleven. Brad didn't want to help him—it was against protocol—but I thought, this is just a little kid. How would I feel if my daughter was thirsty and some jerk didn't give her a drink?"

April blinked. "I didn't know you have a daughter," she said.

Randall looked up, surprised. "Yeah, I do. She's a little older than you, married, two children. You dropped me at her house that one time." He looked away.

"What happened with the boy?" April asked, partially because she wanted to know and partially because she could sense that Randall didn't want to talk about his daughter.

Randall swallowed, and his fingers tightened around Rex's fur. "Our canteens were empty—we were almost done with our shift—so I walked back to the patrol station to refill mine. I got five steps away when the explosion went off. Threw me clean off my feet. I was the lucky one. My partner..." he trailed off.

April was silent. She thought back to that night. She'd been so caught up in her own reaction to finding Andre that she hadn't paid much attention to Randall. But he'd been freaked out too, hadn't he? Rex had had to calm him down, much like he wa doing with her now,

"Why are you here, Randall?"

Randall scratched his stubbly chin. "Mostly to make sure you're okay."

"Mostly?"

"Well, I know how easy it is to fall into something and not be able to get out of it. I'm still not out of it all the way." He looked at her pointedly. "So are you okay?"

"I'm sick."

By the look he gave her, Randall was not convinced. He looked like he might say something else, then nodded. "I'm around if you need me."

He rose, and before he could leave, April asked, "Do you think I should go back?"

He turned towards her. "What do you think?"

"I don't know. I feel sick whenever I think about it. I don't know if I can."

Randall nodded, and stood. "I'll support you whatever you decide to do. Take your time, but the longer you wait, the harder it will be." He stood up. "I'll see you soon either way."

"Bye," April said, but he'd already closed the door. She could hear the occasional murmur from the living room. Gram must have made good on her promise of serving him tea.

She sighed. She'd already made her choice, hadn't she? She'd chosen to fight for the gate, and now she needed to keep to that decision. She tried to tell herself that if she had let Thaddeus take the gate, even more people would have been hurt.

But thinking this didn't make her feel better. That was a numbers game, and Andre hadn't been a number.

~~~

April sat in her car, staring up at the library. It seemed ominous now, no longer just an average brick building barely worth noticing. Maybe she should just start the engine and go home.

"April!"

April turned towards the sound of her name to see Becky hurrying towards her. She sighed and got out of the car.

"Hi, Becky." April tried to smile, but she could tell by the look on Becky's face that it wasn't convincing. "Do I look that bad?" April asked.

"You look... tired," Becky said kindly. "Are you sure you're feeling well enough to come back? It's been tight with Clara covering the third-floor desk, especially with Braddy Evers Day coming up, but we can manage."

"Braddy Evers Day?" April asked.

"You know," Becky said, "From *The First Adventure of Braddy Evers?* We're having a themed festival in the library next weekend. It's in the events calendar."

"Oh, right." April hadn't read *The First Adventure of Braddy Evers,* unlike everyone else in the world. Even though the book was written like, a hundred years ago or something, everyone still loved it. There were even movies and television series based on it. April hadn't even seen those.

"Andre being gone doesn't help, either," Becky said, her voice falling a little.

"Andre's gone?" April said, trying to sound surprised. In one of the messages Dorian had left for her, he'd said, "maintenance took care of everything." Thankfully, he hadn't elaborated on what that meant, exactly. What had they told everyone? She probably should have called and asked Dorian what the story was.

Becky's eyes widened. "No one told you? Crap, I'm sorry. Andre hasn't shown up for work since Friday. The police went over to his house after a few days. According to them it looked like Andre had just packed a bag and left. Can you believe that?"

"No, I can't."

"Me, neither," Becky said. "I tried to put up missing person flyers in the library but Barbara caught wind of it and nixed it. She doesn't want any more drama after Mae's death and the gas leak debacle."

Uh oh. "You don't believe he left?"

"Andre wasn't the type to leave. I know that because his wife left him a few years ago and took their son. He always talked about how cruel it was for her to just disappear." Becky looked sidelong at her. "What do you think?"

"I don't think I knew him well enough to say for sure," April said. Becky seemed to accept this answer. They started to walk into the building.

"I was the last person to see him," Becky said. "We were walking to our cars, and mine was closer to the door. He waved to me and said, 'see you on Monday.' Why would he say that if he was planning on leaving?"

April's eyes prickled. Andre had left that night totally expecting to come back. "I don't know, Becky," April said, sounding more forceful than she intended. "Maybe he was trying to throw you off the trail."

"What?" Becky stopped walking in front of the welcome desk and turned to face her. "I thought you'd be on my side. Everyone else is just concerned with not causing a fuss. What if Andre's hurt? What if he needs our help? What if we do nothing and something worse happens?"

She looked at April earnestly, waiting for her to say something. But what could she say? Andre was dead. She shouldn't have come back.

"I don't know."

Becky let out a disgusted breath and walked away. April didn't call after her. There was nothing to say.

April's legs felt like they were made of lead as she slowly climbed the staircase. She stopped on the landing between the second and third floors. If she went up any higher, she'd see the spot on the floor where Andre had been. Would the blood stain still be there? Would she find a note on her desk about red Kool-aid?

She fought the urge to vomit. She closed her eyes and held a hand over her mouth. She couldn't get sick. If she did, they might send her home again. If that happened, she'd never come back.

But maybe that was better. Did she really want to come back here again? Yes, she decided. If she didn't, it meant Andre had died for no reason.

She forced herself to mount the last few stairs. She looked directly at the spot on the floor where she'd seen Andre. She didn't want to try to avoid it. It was better to get it over with.

The floor was clean, not even the slightest trace of blood. Had they entirely replaced the floor boards? She didn't think blood stains came out of hardwood.

Or maybe the maintenance person had magic cleaning abilities. Nothing would surprise her anymore.

The air inside Mae's office was stale after being closed up for a week. She retrieved the stack of mail from the slot outside of the door then closed it behind her and shut the blinds that looked out into the library. The darkness was comforting, the only light coming from the window behind her desk.

It seemed like only a few minutes before she had to go out to the reference desk. A large stand—the kind normally used to hold oversized dictionaries—sat out in front of the desk with a book from the Werner collection sitting on top of it.

"What's this?" she asked Janet.

"It's a first edition copy of *The First Adventure of Braddy Evers*," Janet explained. "Since we've agreed to better utilize items from the Werner collection, I thought we could have it on display to drum up excitement for Braddy Evers Day. First editions of this book are very rare, especially ones in such good condition. I was just printing off a sign."

She held up a sheet of paper. Printed on it in Times New Roman font were the words "First edition copy of *The First Adventure of Braddy Evers!* Join us for Braddy Evers Day for tea, screenings of the blockbuster movies, and other groundling fun!" The date and hours of the festival were listed at the bottom.

April eyed the book. She'd have to be especially watchful to make sure that no one took the book and left it open somewhere in the library.

Janet was looking at her expectantly, so April tried to smile. "Good idea."

Janet's face erupted into a grin. "I'm glad you think so! Why do the downstairs librarians get to have all the fun?" As she taped up the sign, she chattered away about using the collection to its fullest potential. April was glad when Janet finally left. She wanted to be alone.

About halfway through her shift, the phone rang. April picked up the receiver.

"You've reached the Werner Room. April speaking."

"Hello, Ms. Walker."

April closed her eyes. "What do you want, Thaddeus?"

"Just to check in on you. You haven't been at work in quite a while."

Unless he'd been calling the library every day—which she doubted—Thaddeus must be watching her, or at least watching the library. She shouldn't be surprised.

"I was truly sorry to hear about the security guard."

She gripped the phone so tight that the grooves in the plastic bit into her skin. "How do you know about that?"

"While we can't go inside the library outside of business hours, we're still keeping tabs on you. Our reports show that the security guard went in, but never came out." He paused. "Or at least he didn't *walk* out. Do you know how they disposed of the body?"

She shook her head. Her entire body was numb. "No."

"That's probably best. If the authorities find out, the less you know the better off you'll be."

"Are you threatening me?" Would Thaddeus call the police?

Thaddeus laughed, a short, mirthless sound. "My organization prefers that law enforcement be kept ignorant of this situation. In fact, we will do everything within our influence to keep them away from it. No, I'm not threatening you."

"What, then? Just a happy chat?"

"I'm calling to extend an invitation."

"Invitation?"

"My superiors were impressed by your resourcefulness. You've proven yourself someone they'd rather have as an ally than an enemy."

"Why would I join you? Didn't my kicking your ass make my position clear?"

Pause. "I expected the security guard's death would have opened your eyes to the dangers of the portal. You must realize that if you had kept your word he'd still be alive."

Tears blurred her vision, but she blinked them away. "Screw you."

Thaddeus ignored her outburst. "Despite your betrayal, I still believe you're an ignorant girl thrown into a situation above her pay grade. I don't think you deserve what's about to come down on your head. I implore you to stop this before someone else gets hurt. Don't take this offer lightly, Ms. Walker, as it will be your last chance." He paused, letting his words sink in. "Take some time to think it over. You have my card." The line went dead.

As closing time approached, April had the uneasy feeling that something was wrong. At eight fifteen she realized what it was: Andre wasn't there to make the end of night announcement. She grabbed the walkie talkie off its cradle and started to make her rounds.

There were now only a few weeks to go until finals, and the number of students at the tables had increased exponentially. The only non-student in the room was Randall, who sat at his usual table closest to the reference desk. He hadn't said anything when he came in, only nodded in her direction. They had an unspoken agreement to interact as little as possible while the library was open. She'd felt his worried eyes on her all night.

She walked around, letting the patrons know the library was closing. When she got back to Randall she said, "Do you mind staying after tonight?"

He nodded. "Whatever you need."

"Thanks. Just wait in my office, okay?" Not that Andre would be coming around to check.

At eight thirty-one Becky's voice came over the walkie talkie. "Is everything clear?"

Subdued murmurs issued from the walkie talkie. April pressed the green button. "The third floor is empty. I'll see all of you tomorrow."

Several voices bade her farewell. Becky's wasn't among them. Five minutes later April and Randall were the only people left in the building. Randall exited her office, Rex shaking himself off.

April smiled a little as the dog came over to greet her. "How can you be so sure he won't make any noise and give you away?"

Randall shrugged. "I found him over in Afghanistan. He started following me around one day, even on patrol. If ever there was a dog that knows when to keep quiet, it's this one." His smile turned serious. "Are you sure you want to do this tonight? Coming back to work was a big step in itself. You can wait to do this."

She shook her head. "I don't know if I'm ready but... if I don't do it now I'm not sure I ever will."

Randall nodded, but he still looked worried. "Don't push yourself too much."

"I'm fine."

They sat in silence until the grandfather clock started to chime. She rose and walked over to the gate to watch it open. Dorian waited on the other side, his eyes widening as he saw her. He stepped through before the gate was opened all the way.

He stopped in front of her. "I thought I wouldn't see you again."

"Me, too," April said.

"Are you okay? What made you come back?"

"I don't know," she said, squinting. "Randall came to see me yesterday, and I just thought, 'If I don't go back now, I don't think I'll ever do it.' And here I am."

Dorian looked over at Randall. "You talked to her?"

"I didn't do it for you."

Rex started to growl. His nose pointed to the west wall, the one that faced the parking lot.

"That's strange. He usually doesn't growl," Randall said, and headed towards the window. His eyes widened as he looked out. "We've got company."

April and Dorian walked over to the window. A figure in a long overcoat with the collar popped up to obscure his face even though it was dark out as he approached the main entrance. He wore a bowler hat on his head.

"Is it Thaddeus?" April said, her heart pounding. "I thought he couldn't come here!"

"He can't," Dorian said. "You're safe. It's not Thaddeus."

As safe as Andre? April thought, but Dorian continued before she could say the words out loud.

"I invited him here. He's a friend."

"A friend?" April asked.

Dorian nodded. "A wizard—kind of. He put the spell on the library that keeps the collectors out. It put a huge target on his back, though. He's been in hiding ever since. After last week's events I thought it would be prudent to discuss heightened security, so I attempted to contact him. I wasn't sure he even got my message."

The man looked up at them and waved. April tried to focus on his face and found that she couldn't.

"I'll let him in," Dorian said, and he went downstairs. When he came back the man was with him.

"April, Randall, this is Barty Nagles."

"Bartholomew," the man corrected. "Warlock extraordinaire." He extended his hand, and April took it. She tried to concentrate on his features but again found it difficult. Despite this he looked familiar, though every time she felt close to remembering where she recognized him from the thought slipped away. It was like having a word stuck on the tip of her tongue, but with his face.

"Oh, sorry," Barty said apologetically. He removed the bowler hat, a mass of messy strawberry-blond locks falling out as he did. As soon as the hat was off his head, the overcoat disappeared revealing worn jeans, sneakers, and a faded black polo covered in powdery stains in the shapes of fingers. he was in his late twenties or early thirties.

"Pretty cool, huh?" Barty said, lifting the bowler hat. "I found it in England. A cap of anonymity, they call it. Putting it on makes the wearer's face nearly impossible to remember. I wear it to keep under the collectors' radar. If they knew I was back in town..." he shivered.

"That's one blessing in all of this," Dorian said. "We haven't heard from them since bested them last week."

"Not quite." April told them about Thaddeus' phone call.

"Did he threaten you?" Randall asked after she finished.

April shook her head. "No. He offered me a job."

"A job?" Barty asked. "Why?"

"They're trying to get her on their side," Dorian said. "A smart tactic, if it works."

Randall was the first to say anything else. "Are you considering it?"

She thought for a moment. "No." It was true.

Barty shivered. "These collectors are a bad deal. They killed my grandfather, and they'll kill me if they get a chance. You, too. Now that you're the Pagewalker, you're just magic scum to them. They have something up their sleeves, mark my words."

"You're probably right."

Dorian looked thoughtful. "Barty, can you set up some magical protection for April that will work when she's not in the library? Just in case."

Barty thought for a moment. "I can't work a full-on protection spell. I hardly managed it the first time, and I had several powerful items I no longer have access to, thanks to the collectors. I can probably work up a warning amulet.

It won't do anything in the way of protection, but at least you'll know they're coming."

"How long will that take?" Dorian asked.

"I should have it by tomorrow. I'm working the day shift, so I can come as soon as the library closes."

April snapped her fingers, remembering where she recognized Barty from. "You're the delivery driver for Nemo's Pizza!"

Dorian turned to look at Barty with disgust. "You're delivering pizza?"

Barty's cheeks turned hot pink. "It's not like studying arcane magic pays the bills. And I'm surprised you know what pizza is, Mister nineteenth-century London."

Dorian rolled his eyes. "I've been coming into this world for almost thirty years, your time," he said. "And of all the things your world has to offer, pizza is one of the best."

"I thought the collectors wiped all the warlocks and other magic-wielders out," April said.

"They did for the most part," Barty said with a sad nod. "I'm sure there are some left, but they're the ones who are good at hiding. Thus, the cap." He proffered the bowler hat.

"Barty," Dorian said with a warning tone in his voice.

Barty sighed. "Fine. I'm not really a warlock. My grandfather was, though. The collectors got him nearly fifty years ago. I never knew him."

"But you know how to cast spells?" April said.

"Yes and no. I found his grimoires about a decade ago."

"What's a grimoire?"

"Like a spellbook. I was able to make some of the magic work... kind of. It's like following a recipe when you don't know how to cook. Some are easy, others not so much."

"And the collectors are after you?"

Barty nodded. "They didn't know I existed until I cast the spell on the library. That's pretty impressive magic." Barty thrust his chest out. "But it got me on their list."

"And you've been delivering pizza ever since?" Dorian said. "I thought you went into hiding."

"I did," Barty said a tad defensively. "Minneapolis wasn't safe for me any more. I couldn't go back to school, and I didn't want to endanger my family. So I went to Europe in search of magic."

"You've been traveling the world looking for magical objects like that hat-of-whatever?" Randall asked.

"Cap of anonymity," Barty corrected. "That's part of it. More importantly I've been looking for a mentor—someone who could teach me how to cook, not just follow a recipe." He shook his head. "I haven't found them. Maybe they really are all dead."

"Where are these grimoires now?" Randall asked. "Maybe there's something in there that can help us."

Barty shook his head. "That's partially why I'm here. Before I went into hiding, Mae took them and hid them in one of the books. We figured it was the safest place for them, seeing as the collectors can't access the gate, and even if they do finding them in all the books would be like looking for a needle in a haystack."

"Which book are they in?" April asked.

Barty shrugged. "I don't know. We decided it was best that I not know in case they caught up with me. I was hoping that she told you before she passed."

April shook her head. "There wasn't time. Do you know, Dorian?"

Dorian shook his head. He looked down. "She never shared that with me. There were things she kept from me for various reasons."

"Hold on," April said. She'd felt a sudden burst of insight, though she wasn't sure where it had come from. There was something she was missing, something she needed to put together... She walked to Mae's office, not sure what she was looking for until she saw Mae's planner sitting on the desk. She opened it to the page where it said, *For Barty: Turner, S. pg 113.*

Dorian looked at the note. "It's possible. She must have taken something of roughly equal size back with her. Let's see... Turner..." he walked towards the shelf where the Werner books were kept and pulled one down.

"*A Country Romance* by M. Turner," he read. "If you were going to hide something in a book, this one seems like a good choice. Probably just men and woman courting each other. Less chance of being hung or beaten to death. What's the page?"

She read out the number to him, and he carefully lifted only the bottom corner of the book to find the page before he opened the cover. The crack appeared in the window and widened to reveal a field of heather and wildflowers. A ridge of trees lined the edge of the field off in the distance.

Dorian's eyes traveled across the page. "It's a setting description. No one to bother us."

"Can I see that?" Randall reached out his hand and Dorian handed him the book. Randall examined the text. "What would happen if I turned the page now?"

Dorian shook his head. "Not advisable. The portal will change to the next page, but your ears will be ringing for days from all the racket. It sends shockwaves out, sometimes even cracks the wall. I'm surprised no one has commented on the number of 'micro-quakes' this building has seen."

Randall looked down at the book as though it were a bomb.

"Shall we?" Dorian asked.

"I wouldn't say no to finding my grimoires," Barty said.

"You ready for this, April?" Randall asked. "It's okay if you're not."

Was she? April looked down at the book in Randall's hands. *Don't give yourself a chance to change your mind.*

While she was looking at the book, she noticed a familiar darkness near the spine. "Is that ink rot?" she asked.

Dorian looked grimly at the book and nodded. "No one's been maintaining the collection, so it's spreading faster. While we're inside, we should look for the rot and clean up as much of it as possible. If you're up for it," he added the last part hastily.

"Let's do it," she said.

"If we're taking something back with us," Dorian said, "We need something of similar size to leave behind in its place."

April walked over to the discard cart where library patrons left the books they'd decided not to check out. She picked up a copy of the second most recent James Patterson hardback that someone had brought up from the second floor.

"We have about twenty copies of this one. They'll never miss it." She looked at Randall. "Want to come with? You haven't been through the gate before.

Rex, too." She held her breath. She hoped he would come. His presence made her feel calmer, more capable.

He looked at the gate. "Does it hurt?"

April shook her head. "It feels weird, though."

"Sure."

Barty rubbed the back of his neck. "I'll stay here. I've been through once before, and... when you know how hard it is to produce even a small spell, something that's this powerful is unsettling." He paused, then added, "I'll watch the book."

Dorian nodded his approval. He turned to April, his eyebrows raised. "Well?"

She breathed out. All they had to do was look for Barty's grimoires and deal with the ink rot. The ink rot in *One Thousand and One Nights* had dispersed easily at her touch. This should be a piece of cake. "Let's do it."

She went first through the gate, followed by Randall and then Dorian. Randall's face sported a look of trepidation as he passed through behind her.

He glanced around. "I'll be damned," he said. "It is real." Then he bent over and vomited. April patted him on the shoulder.

There was a yip as Rex jumped through the portal behind them. He sniffed at Randall.

"You okay?" April asked.

It took Randall a moment to nod. "Yeah," he said. "It's just... this makes me wonder if I really am crazy."

"Me, too." She said. She watched him for a few more seconds to make sure he was okay, then turned to see where the gate had materialized. Instead of being in a doorway like every other time she'd seen it, it was between two trees at the edge of the forest behind them.

"It makes do with what it has if there aren't any doors around," Dorian explained.

April nodded, gazing back through the veil. Barty waved to her. She stepped to one side, and he disappeared, along with the rest of the gate—it was only visible when viewed straight-on.

"We have to be careful to remember where it is," she said.

Dorian nodded. "Mae and I once lost the gate while we were in *Little Red Riding Hood* in *The Blue Fairy Book*. It wasn't fun trying to locate it again amongst all the trees. Not to mention the pack of wolves that was stalking us."

"I have an idea," Randall said. He walked over to a small log near the edge of the wood and dragged it in front of the gate.

"Good idea." April said. "Where do you think Mae hid the grimoires? Do you think she buried them?"

Dorian shrugged. "It's hard to imagine Mae digging a hole even several years ago, but I don't see anywhere else where she might have hidden them."

April looked around. The field was huge. "If we split up, this will go faster. Why don't you guys look for the grimoires, and I'll look for the rot?"

"Fine," Dorian said. "Just wait for us before you do anything with the rot, should you find it."

They separated, and she began walking around the edge of the clearing. Dorian had said that the rot usually materialized within sight of the place where the gate materialized, but she couldn't see any.

One edge of the field sloped upwards. As she made her way up the incline, a small stone cottage with a thatched roof came into view. She was suddenly overcome with the certainty that what they were searching for was inside the cottage. It reminded her of how she'd known to look in Mae's planner.

Dorian had said Mae would always get hunches and bursts of intuition. Was that happening to her? Was the gate influencing her, affecting her? She couldn't help but feel violated.

She tried to ignore the feeling as she stared at the cottage. Should she go in by herself, or get Randall and Dorian? Finally she decided to go back down and get them.

Dorian and Randall were arguing when she made her way back around the edge of the woods towards them.

"She must have buried it," Randall said.

"There's no way Mae could have buried it. Maybe she hid them in a tree."

"If they were hidden in a tree, they would be ruined by rainwater and bugs. Mae was too smart for that."

"Guys, stop arguing," April said when she was close enough for them to hear her without her yelling.

"Did you find the rot?" Dorian asked.

She shook her head. "The field is totally clean, but there's a house on the other side of that hill."

Two minutes later they stood in front of the cottage. Much like the meadow, the surrounding area was deserted.

Dorian rapped his knuckles against the door. No response.

Randall glanced through the dirty window. "Empty."

They pushed the door open, surprised to find it unlocked. They stepped cautiously inside. Though the place was empty, it was obviously lived in. There was a stack of firewood by the hearth, and the tang of woodsmoke and cooking grease mixed in the air. It felt as though the cottage's inhabitants had stepped outside and would return momentarily.

They looked around, checking underneath the bed in the corner, up in the storage loft, and in a large trunk in the corner near the door. The search turned up no ink rot and nothing remotely book-like.

"Nothing," Dorian said, frustrated. "Mae wrote down this book and this page for a reason! There must be something we're not seeing."

"Wait," Randall said. He stomped his sneaker-clad foot on the wooden floor. The sound echoed dully. "It's hollow."

"A cellar in a hovel like this?" Dorian said.

They pulled up the rug covering the floor. There was a trapdoor loosely cut into the wood. They lifted it up, revealing a dark cellar. The odor of damp earth and root vegetables drifted up to them.

They stared into the hole. "Should have brought a flashlight," Randall said.

"I got it." April pulled her cell phone from her back pocket and activated the flashlight app. She shone the light down in the hole. It illuminated steps fashioned from rough blocks of stone that led into the darkness.

"Ladies first," she said, and before they could protest she descended the stairs. When she got to the bottom she directed the flashlight around her in a circle.

Dorian's face appeared in the square of light up above her head. "What do you see?" he asked.

"The room's about ten by ten feet, though most of the space is taken up by vegetables. Nothing looks particularly grimoire-y. Hold on..." the light fell on a burlap mound that looked a little too square. She walked over to it and pulled away the burlap. Underneath was a stack of leather-bound books. She opened one up. Hand-written inside the front cover was *C.M. Nagles—Grimoire.*

"They're here." She walked back to the hole and handed the book up to Dorian.

"Barty will be chuffed," he said. "Don't forget to leave the replacement."

She placed the James Patterson book on top of the pile and recovered the grimoires with the burlap, then climbed back up the ladder. Before she could step out of the way for Dorian to head down, Rex began to growl, his eyes trained on the back window of the cottage.

"Maybe Barty followed us?" April said.

"Not likely," Dorian said. "He's terrified of the gate." He walked over to the window, and his eyes widened.

"What?" She and Randall moved towards the window to see what he was looking at.

"I think we've found the source of the ink rot. Or, more accurately, it found us."

A small boy wearing plain worn clothes stood on the edge of the treeline. At first April thought his face was in shadow from the trees because she couldn't make out his features. But he was too far away from the tree line. His face was gone, replaced by feathery dark tendrils that trailed down his throat and beneath the collar of his shirt.

"That's ink rot?" Randall said. "It's horrible. Can he feel it?"

Dorian shook his head. "I don't know."

"Can I help him?" There was something repellant about the thought of touching the boy, but at the same time she wanted to do it. Part of her hoped that Dorian would say it wasn't possible. Immediately she felt bad for the thought. She should want to help the boy.

Dorian looked unsure. "It's further along than I would have guessed. I'm not sure you're ready for this much."

"What happens if I don't do anything? Does it get worse?"

Dorian nodded. "It will spread until it consumes the rest of this world. The further it spreads, the faster it happens."

"I have to try, then," she said.

"Ms. Walker—" Dorian said, his voice uneasy.

"I'm doing it."

A tense silence filled the cottage. She added, "Isn't this what you want me to do? Let me do it."

Dorian stared into her eyes for several moments, then nodded. "Very well."

They closed the trapdoor before leaving the cottage. As they walked around to the back of the house, the little boy's head tilted to the side, like an inquisitive dog.

"I think that's a good sign," Dorian said. "There's still something in there."

"What do I do?"

"The same thing you did last time—contact with your bare skin."

"Right." She walked to the boy, and as she did, the boy's head turned towards her. She wondered how he was tracking her movement. His eyes were obscured by the inky blackness. As she got closer she realized that his features appeared totally smooth. Was it an illusion, the rot so black that it made light and shadow indistinguishable from one another, or had it actually eaten away at his face?

"Hi," she said when she was five feet away from him. Except for the head-tilt, he hadn't moved. "I'm going to touch you, okay? You'll feel better afterwards." She tried to talk the way Becky talked to the kids at the library.

She waited for the boy to react, but he only kept his head tilted towards her. It wasn't like he was looking at her, exactly; it was more like a flower tilted towards the sun. Unseeing but responsive all the same. She approached, placing her hand on his forehead as though testing whether he had a fever. Unlike the dessicated ink rot she'd encountered in *One Thousand and One Nights,* the substance covering the boy's features was smooth and shiny, like actual ink.

As her hand came into contact with it, the edges of the black substance turned to powder and flaked off, but the majority remained wet and cold. It stuck to her fingers, and when she pulled her hand away it came away with it, like gum stuck to the bottom of a shoe.

"It didn't work!" she yelled back to Dorian and Randall, her voice high-pitched. She tried to step backwards, but the rot clung to her hands and stretched with her.

"Concentrate," Dorian yelled back. "It's further along than what you saw before. It will take more energy, more will."

Concentrate? She didn't think she could. She quieted the panic rising like hot bile in her chest and focused on the oozing substance on her hand, but then it seemed to be eating its way up her arm...

She squealed and again attempted to pull her hand free, but the ink held fast. "Help me!"

"We have to help her," Randall said, and there was a scuffle behind her as Dorian attempted to hold him back.

"There's nothing you can do. She has to do it herself." he said. "She chose this. This is what being the Pagewalker *is.*"

His words must have convinced Randall, because he didn't come to save her. The ooze continued its slow ascent up her arm. If she was the only one who could stop this stuff, then she was a goner.

Then she looked at the little boy. Without being able to see his face it was difficult to gauge his age, but from his size he appeared no more than eight. If she didn't stop the ink rot, what would happen to him? She had to try.

She concentrated on the place where his face should have been. She made herself pretend that she could see his face, two little blue eyes and a small button nose, thin lips...

She realized she wasn't pretending anymore. The features were there, pushing up through the rot. The rot itself grew dry until it cracked like parched clay, then scaled off as the boy gained control of his movements.

The powdery remainder of the rot blew away in a light breeze, including what had been on her arm.

She looked down at her arm and then at the boy. She did it!

She grabbed the boy's shoulders and checked his face and arms for any remaining traces of the rot.

"Are you okay?" she asked him.

The boy's eyes were the size and shape of silver dollars. He slipped from her grasp and ran into the woods. Happy whupping erupted behind her.

"You did it!" Randall yelled. He and Dorian ran towards her.

Dorian smiled. "I knew you could."

She was about to tell him that she was glad he thought so because she hadn't been so sure, but then her knees folded beneath her. She grabbed his shoulders to keep from crumpling completely to the ground.

He grabbed her by the waist to steady her. "You're okay," he told her, but his brow was furrowed. "Dispersing the ink rot takes a lot of energy. You're not used to it. It's like building muscle. You just overextended yourself."

She nodded, trusting that he was right. She felt like she could sleep for a week.

"Let's get you back to the library."

"What about the rest of the books?"

"We know where they are now. We'll come back for them later."

Barty was ecstatic when Randall handed him the dusty tome. He kept touching the pages as though he couldn't believe they were real.

They were sitting in the little reading area in the corner. April was lying on the couch, her coat laid over her lap. She sipped tea that Randall had ventured down to the break room to make. They'd dipped into the supplies for Braddy Evers Day.

"You're lucky this place hasn't gotten surveillance cameras yet," he said as he handed her the steaming mug.

She snorted. "The city won't even shell out for new carpets. There's no way they're going to pay for security cameras."

Barty flipped through the grimoire happily. "There's archaic knowledge here that the collectors have all but wiped out. When can you get the others?"

Dorian spoke up. "I think it's best to have only one volume of the grimoire here at a time. What if the collectors got ahold of them?"

Barty looked disappointed. "You're right," he said. "I should focus on this one, anyway."

They fell into a long silence during which April almost dozed off. Then Randall said, "What *is* ink rot? What causes it?"

Barty cleared his throat importantly. "From what Mae told me, Oswald Werner was interested in rekindling the magic that the collectors have all but wiped out. I think he may have found the gate itself, but not its keys."

"Keys?" April asked.

"Magical items that tell the gate where to open up to," Dorian said.

"Like magical GPS coordinates?" Randall asked.

"Basically. The keys were all taken by the collectors. So Oswald had the gate and managed to restore it, but he needed keys to be able to use it."

"So he, what, made his own keys out of books?"

"Precisely. But something went wrong. Either he didn't have all the information he needed to do it correctly, or things like books were never meant to be keys in the first place. So they deteriorate if not maintained."

"What happens if we don't stop the rot?"

Dorian grimaced. "There's a certain point where the effects are irreversible. The ink eats everything."

April tried to wrap her head around what that meant. "So everything just disappears?"

"Not quite," Dorian said. "It's not pretty."

April sat up straight. "Wait—so it's happened before?"

Dorian nodded.

"I want to see," April said. She set aside her empty mug and pushed her coat onto the floor. She rose to her feet, swaying as she did.

A second later, Dorian was at her side, again holding her around the waist. It felt good, comforting, and she pushed him away. She didn't want to feel comforted.

"You're spent," he said, allowing himself to be pushed away though he still hovered protectively nearby, ready to catch her.

"He's right," Randall said. "You can barely stand. You need to rest."

"*I want to see,*" she said. She looked Dorian in the eyes. "Please."

"Okay," Dorian said after a few seconds, though he sounded unsure. "We'll look through the veil, but we're not going in. It's too dangerous." He walked back to Mae's office. "We keep the black books under the floorboards in Mae's office."

He came out holding a book. It was the color of tar, as though the entire thing had been held over a flame for hours, slowly collecting smoke. The title was completely obscured.

"What book is it?" April asked.

Dorian shook his head. "Impossible to tell. Not that it matters, though. Anything that made this world what it was is gone."

They walked over to the gate, Randall holding April's elbow to steady her.

"Ready?" Dorian asked. She nodded. He opened the book. The pages were just as black as the cover. She was surprised it left no residue on Dorian's fingers.

The gate began to open. The room was filled not with the familiar human sounds and smells that she'd grown accustomed to encountering with the gate.

Instead, it smelled like rot—all kinds of it, the rot of old vegetables, old wood, ancient paper. Even decaying flesh.

"I can see where it got its name," Randall said. He pulled the neck of his shirt up over his nose. Rex sniffed cautiously at the air. The fur along his back stood up.

It was hard to make out what lay beyond the gate. The light was dim, like sunlight filtered through thick layers of glistening black smog.

But then parts of the blackness began to shift. The substance absorbed the light and made everything appear flat and dimensionless. She recognized square shapes that had once been buildings and smaller, bulgier shapes that might have been carriages or cars.

And yet smaller shapes that were once people, too. They were all featureless like the boy had been, with only black mounds where their noses should have been and indents for their eyes. They were walking around, but their movements were slow and jerky. At first, they seemed unaware of the gate, but then a shudder passed through them, and their faces snapped towards it.

"Can they see us?" Randall asked. His grip on her elbow tightened. He stepped backwards away from the gate, pulling her with him.

"No," Dorian said. "But they can sense that something hasn't been taken over by the rot. At least, that was Mae's theory."

The closest figure began to shamble towards them, the rest following closely behind. It leaned towards the portal as though to examine it, but how could it, when it didn't have any eyes to see with, or even a nose to smell with?

Then it reached out towards them as though to probe the veil with its hand.

There was a snap as Dorian closed the book in his hands. The gate began to close, and the ink-person leaned back away from it. The last thing April saw before the gate closed was the hunch of the creature's shoulders.

"I think we can all agree we don't want them passing through the veil," Dorian said.

Barty and Randall murmured their assent. Their voices were tense, frightened.

"We need to help them," April said. "They're miserable!"

Dorian shook his head. "It's impossible. Mae tried and it almost killed her. And that was when she was younger and stronger."

"How many black books are there?" April asked.

"About a dozen. Most have been like that for a long time. Mae didn't know about the ink rot at first, so she didn't know she needed to maintain the collection." There was a long pause.

Finally Randall spoke. "I think that's enough for tonight. We'll meet again tomorrow. For now, April needs to rest."

Barty nodded. "I'll be here."

Randall turned her slowly around and towards the door. He slipped her coat over her shoulders and grabbed her purse for her.

"You did good," Randall said. "You saved that boy. Let yourself rest. You're no good to anyone without a little sleep."

She allowed herself to be led to the exit, her eyes lingering on the spot where they'd found Andre. So clean, like he'd never even been there.

~~~

Randall drove her car to her grandmother's house and then he and Rex walked back towards the library, reassuring her that he had a place to sleep that night. She wasn't sure she believed him, but she didn't have the energy to argue.

She fell asleep as soon as she crawled under the covers, still in her work clothes. She'd barely bothered to kick off her shoes.

She dreamed that she was back in the open field. A figure stood off in the distance where the boy had been standing. She thought it was the boy again, but it was difficult to tell because it was facing away from her towards the trees.

"I can help you," she called, but the air swallowed her words like she was speaking underwater. She began moving towards the figure, but barely made any progress, like she was walking on a large treadmill that carried her backwards with every step.

Finally she reached the figure, which now stood facing the trees, though she was sure it had been turned the other way a few minutes earlier. It wasn't the boy. It was too large, and the boy hadn't been dressed in a white polo and black pants...

"Let me help you," she said again. She placed her hand on the figure's shoulder, turning it around. It was Andre. But hadn't it always been Andre? She had a moment to see his lifeless eyes before the ink rot covered them, and then they were only smooth hollows. Liquid black rot squirted up through his white shirt, soaking through the word *security* embroidered there.

She reached out to touch the ink rot. Her heart beat hard in her chest. If she could just make it go away, everything would be fine again. But the rot was too far gone. She'd arrived too late... if she touched it, it would consume her as well.

Still, she reached for it.

"Don't."

The word came from behind her. She turned, expecting to see Dorian or Randall. Instead, the genie stood there. He smirked, an expression she found oddly comforting.

"I have to," she said. "I need to save him..." she turned back to Andre, but he was gone.

She turned back to the genie, about to ask him where Andre had gone, to insist they look for him. But the genie reached out and wrapped his arms around her shoulders.

His touch was hot, and it burned away all of her concerns, fears, and worries. She felt suddenly tired, like she could fall asleep even in her dream.

If she dreamt more than that, she did not remember it when she woke the next morning.

Chapter Three

April relieved Janet from the reference desk. Janet was bebriefing her on the agenda for the day when a woman and a boy walked into the Werner Room.

The boy was no more than twelve years old, Latino, thickly built, and familiar.

"Who is that?" she asked, though she already knew.

Janet looked out. "Oh, crap. That's Andre's ex-wife. She's been in here at least three times since last Thursday, grilling the staff about Andre." She slid out of her chair. "And you're the only person she hasn't harassed yet. Lucky you."

At that moment the woman was only a few feet away from the desk. Janet smiled at her. "Hi, Ms. Beauchamp. It's lovely to see you again. I was just leaving, but April will be happy to help you with whatever you need."

She backed away, and when Mrs. Beauchamp's back was turned to her she mouthed *sorry* behind her back, then turned and practically sprinted towards the stairs.

"Are you April Walker?" the woman asked, a hand on her hip.

April nodded. "Yes, ma'am. I was very sorry to hear about—"

The woman waved away April's words. "Save it. I know my ex-husband. He skipped town, probably to get out of paying child support." She reached back behind her and grabbed her son's arm, pulling him forward. "Do you see this kid? His father's son, every inch of him. And he eats like him, too. How I am supposed to pay for all of that plus clothes and school supplies and everything else? Not to mention that I had to take time off work to come look for him."

The boy looked down at his feet, his jaw hard. Splotches of scarlet erupted across his face. How could this woman say these things about her own son in front of him?

"What's your name?" April asked the boy.

"Rico," the boy mumbled. His voice was a softer version of his mother's intense New England bray mixed with Andre's Latin lilt. Once his voice changed April had no doubt it would match his father's deep bass timbre.

April turned back to Rico's mom. "Andre didn't seem like the kind of guy who'd do that," she said. One of Andre's favorite topics was his son, and how he wished he could see him more than he did.

"Oh, everyone thinks that Andre's such a saint because I was the one who left him. Well I'll tell you what, he didn't deserve me." She narrowed her eyes. "They said that you were here the last night that he worked. Did you notice anything strange? Maybe he said something to you, something about going on a trip? Maybe meeting a girlfriend?"

April tried to keep her face neutral. *Just stick to the facts,* she thought to herself. What had Andre done that night? To be honest, she hadn't paid much attention. It had been just a regular night until it wasn't, and she'd been on a high from passing Barbara's test. That all seemed so far away.

"Nothing seemed out of the ordinary," she said. "He made the fifteen-minute closing announcement then came up to say good night. He mentioned that he was looking forward to seeing his son that weekend."

Andre hadn't said this that night, but she was sure he'd said it during the day, and she thought it was important for Rico to hear it.

"Hmm," Ms. Beauchamp said. "That's pretty much what everyone else said." She paused, then narrowed her eyes. "You were out the week following his disappearance. I kept calling in to try to talk to you."

April's heart started beating. "I had food poisoning," she said. "I didn't even know that Andre had disappeared until the following Monday when I came back to work."

"You seem nervous."

Damn it. Was she that much of an open book? "Andre was a colleague and a friend. We're all upset."

Mrs. Beauchamp continued to squint, considering April's words. Then she nodded. "Of course. If you think of anything else, please get in touch. We're staying in Andre's apartment while we're in town, so you can call his land line."

April nodded. "I'll keep that in mind."

Rico glanced back at her as they walked away. April didn't like the way he was looking at her, as though he was waiting for something. Ms. Beauchamp grabbed her son's wrist and pulled him towards the stairwell.

A few minutes later Becky walked up the stairs carrying a box. She looked around, trying to avoid April's gaze, then seemed resigned to having to talk to her.

"I saw Andre's ex-wife and son come up," she said. "Are they still here?"

"They left a few minutes ago."

"Dang it. I was going to give her Andre's things." She gazed down at the box unhappily. It contained various knickknacks, a coffee-stained mug, a photo of Rico, and the security jacket he sometimes wore around the building.

"They're staying at his apartment," April said. "You can call them there."

"Oh," Becky said. "I'll do that." Her voice was distant, and she didn't hold April's gaze. She must still be upset about what April said in the parking lot the previous afternoon.

After Becky left, April tried to get into the groove of working the reference desk, but she kept thinking about Rico and the way he'd looked back at her before his mother had pulled him away.

If April had let Thaddeus take the gate, then Rico would still have his father.

But was that really fair? If April had let Thaddeus do whatever he was going to do with the gate, then all the people in the books would have died. Even if their worlds wouldn't have been destroyed when Thaddeus decommissioned the gate, then they all would have ended up like those people she'd seen through the veil the previous night. Maybe Thaddeus was right. They weren't real people. But they'd sure seemed like they were. Dorian was real, wasn't he?

But she didn't know any of those other people. None of them except Dorian. She didn't have to look into their children's eyes.

~~~

April, Barty, Randall, and Dorian sat around the coffee table in the sitting area. Barty pulled a small box out of his pocket. The top was stained in splotches of pizza grease. He handed it to her. "It's the amulet," he said.

She opened the box. Inside, wrapped in a paper towel was a rock on a piece of string. It looked like a necklace that a five year old might make for their mother.

"The stone will glow if the collectors are around you and mean you harm," Barty said. He sounded proud.

"Oh," April said. "That's good. Do I have to wear it, or can I keep it in my pocket?"

"It has to be worn around your neck," Barty said. "I know it's not the prettiest thing. I didn't exactly have time to craft a Tiffany's-worthy piece of jewelry. But it will keep you safe."

"Sorry. Thank you." She slipped it over her head. She'd be sure to wear clothes that covered it, anyway.

"Excellent," Dorian said. "Now, there's one more order of business: the ink rot."

April breathed out. "Right. Let's start."

"Start?"

"You said the ink rot has gotten bad since Mae got sick. We need to work on turning that around before it gets worse."

Dorian nodded. "Quite right. I think we should start with the books where it hasn't gotten too bad yet, so you can practice—"

April shook her head. "No. We should start with the worst cases so that they don't become too much to handle."

Dorian shook his head. "I don't think that's a good idea. You're still exhausted from last night. You'll get used to it, of course, but you need time to recover. The boy was too much. I shouldn't have allowed it."

"What would you have done?" April asked. "Just let the rot consume him? Let him turn into one of those... things?" Everyone stared at her. "Being the Pagewalker means being around death and suffering. I get it. But that doesn't mean I have to get used to it."

The others all exchanged glances. Finally, Dorian said, "Well, it would help keep more of the books becoming black—"

April crossed her arms. "If I work hard enough, I can get good enough at this to fix the blackened books, right? You said it's like building muscle."

Dorian cleared his throat. "You should not expect that of yourself. I've seen it nearly kill Mae."

"I can do it," April said.

Dorian rose to his feet. "Don't think that Mae wasn't dedicated," he said. "She did everything in her power to save those books. It's suicidal to assume you can do better."

"I have to," she said. "I have to make Andre's death worth it."

Everyone fell so silent that they could hear the ticking of the grandfather clock. April looked back at it. Nine forty-five. They'd been talking for nearly an hour.

"We're wasting time," she said. "Do you have a record of which books have the worst ink rot?"

Dorian's voice was resigned when he responded. "I keep track of when the ink rot first appears on the books." He reached into his blazer and pulled out a small notebook.

"I didn't know you did that."

"What do you think I do after you go home each night?" He walked over to the shelf and pulled off one of the books. He showed her the cover. *The Scarlet Letter*. She vaguely remembered it being assigned in her high school literature class. She hadn't read the whole thing, but she sort of remembered what it was about. Puritanical New England or something.

"Is this the worst book?" She asked.

"It is the worst one I'm letting you near," Dorian said. "If you feel that's not sufficient, you can choose the book yourself." He tucked the small notebook safely back into his coat.

There wasn't time to argue. "Fine. We'll start there." She pulled the book out of his hand and glanced at the other two.

"Does anyone have a problem with that?"

No one said anything. She walked towards the east wall, and as she did, she heard Dorian whisper to the others, "*Don't worry—she'll be so exhausted that she won't be able to do another...*"

She pretended not to hear him and laid the book open on its spine. Dorian and Randall walked over and flanked her.

"What do you guys think you're doing?"

"We're your backup," Randall said.

Dorian nodded in agreement.

"Just don't slow me down."

Dorian's expression became sour. "I've been doing this since before you were born! *Don't slow me down...*" the last part was muttered in a mockery of her voice.

She looked back at Barty. "Make sure the book stays open."

Randall's skin developed a greenish tinge after they stepped through the gate. He leaned over with his hands on his knees. "I don't think I'll ever get used to that."

Rex sniffed at him to make sure he was alright, and Randall patted his head reassuringly.

"You will." April said. She didn't feel sick at all. She hadn't felt sick the previous night, either. Weird. Maybe she was adapting.

The gate had opened onto a dirt road directly across from a small church. If it weren't for the simple wooden cross on the top, April wouldn't have recognized it as a house of worship. Two women in bonnets chatted as they carried baskets of vegetables up the road. They stared at them as they passed.

"I thought the gate makes us blend in," April said.

"It does," Dorian said. "But there's a couple hundred people living in this area, if that. We stand out as strangers here. If anyone asks, we can tell them we're from a nearby town and are here visiting relatives."

Randall rubbed his chin. "What do you mean, 'it makes us blend in?'"

"Take a look," April said, pointing to a trough of water.

They went and stood next to it. April's reflection was plain and lined, though she didn't think she was much older. She wore a faded black dress and a white bonnet covered her hair.

Randall touched his face. "I'm white," he said. "Not sure how to feel about that."

"The gate's trying to protect you," Dorian said. "Boston was the first city in the Americas to participate in the slave trade."

Randall nodded at this. "What's the plan? Where will we find this rot?"

Dorian gestured around him. "The rot was on these pages, but there might be smaller concentrations of it elsewhere. I think we should split up and check for more. Then we meet up and make a game plan. I'll take everything to the left, Randall, you take everything to the right. April, you check the church."

"What if the rot has spread further than that?" Randall asked.

Dorian shook his head. "In the early stages it generally won't go beyond sight distance of the gate and won't move farther than described in the narrative. For a book like this where all the action takes place in one small area, that makes our job a lot eaiser."

"Good to know. Let's get started," April said.

Dorian nodded up at the church. "You'll probably find the most rot here. Go ahead and take care of it if it's not too advanced. If it's as bad as or worse than yesterday, wait for us."

Randall nodded. "Let's meet back here in fifteen minutes."

Randall and Dorian walked off in their respective directions, and April stood in front of the church. It didn't look like much, just a small gray stone building with a steepled roof. She tried the door. It was open; in fact, there didn't seem to be a lock on it at all.

April's family hadn't been very religious, so she'd only been to church once or twice on Christmas and a few times when she'd spent the night at a friend's house. She'd never considered those churches lavish, but there had at least been an altar and a cross up at the front, and maybe a decorative tapestry or two on the walls. This room was even plainer. Backless benches lined the floor facing a rough-hewn table. The room was lit by candles. She didn't see any ink rot.

A door was behind the table, and a muffled voice came from it, almost chant-like. She couldn't make out the words. A rhythmic *slap slap slap* sound accompanied the chanting, and each slap was punctuated by a hiss of pain. Sometimes, when the *slap* was especially loud the hiss became a muffled cry.

"Hello?" she called towards the room. "Are you okay?"

The chanting and slapping sounds stopped abruptly. A moment of silence was followed by the scraping of wood, and the bang of something being slammed shut.

"Just a minute," a male voice trembled. A few seconds later the door opened and a man stepped out. He adjusted the collar of his off-white shirt, as though he'd just buttoned it. He pulled on a black coat, but not before she saw a hint of red on the shirt. Blood?

"I must beg thy forgiveness," he said. His voice was fluttery and weak, reminiscent of butterflies. "I do not usually have visitors this late and thou have caught me at an... inopportune moment. I was preparing to bed."

He looked like he could use the sleep. The skin beneath his eyes was swollen and dark, like he was recovering from a bad illness. His frame was nearly skeletal. But maybe everyone who lived in Puritanical England was malnourished. It was a hard life, after all.

He examined her face, his brow furrowing. "Thou must accept my apologies," he said. "I do not recognize thy face."

Oh, right. The cover story. "I'm visiting relatives," she said.

"You must be John Goode's cousin visiting from Capeton."

She smiled, glad that she didn't have to supply these details. "That's right. You are the minister of this church?"

The man nodded. "Forgive me for not introducing myself. My name is Arthur Dimmesdale. What brings thee here at this late hour?"

What did bring her there? She couldn't tell him the truth.

When she didn't immediately speak, he said, "Perhaps thou seeks holy counsel?"

Not sure what else to do, she nodded.

"Come, child. There is nothing you can't say to the Lord. It will ease thy spirit's burden."

She struggled to come up with a believable cover story, but he was looking at her expectantly, so she spoke. "I caused someone to die. It was an accident... but my fault, still."

"Hmmm," Dimmesdale said. "That is quite a cross to bear. Have thou spoken to anyone else about this?"

She shook her head. "Everyone thinks it was an accident. It *was* an accident, but..."

Dimmesdale looked down at her, pity in his eyes—and something darker. Empathy? "Thou have done well to bare thy soul. God forgives all if you ask him to, but thou will not find peace until you face the consequences for your actions."

"What?"

"Thou must do penance."

"I'm doing good deeds," she said, "Helping others."

The minister smiled sadly. "Child, good deeds are admirable, but thou wouldst do them anyway, wouldst thou not?"

She hadn't thought of this. If Andre hadn't died, she'd still be clearing up the rot, wouldn't she? So she really wasn't doing anything extra. She nodded, her heart sinking.

"Then what penance art thou really committing? Purifying the body purifies the soul."

A crash outside the church made them both jump. Dimmesdale turned towards the noise.

"Excuse me," he said. "Dogs have been digging through the graveyard these past few nights. I'll chase them off."

She shook her head, clearing it of Dimmesdale's words. She didn't have time to think about all of this, about whether or not he was right. She had a job to do. She walked to the door at the front of the church and pushed the door open. She smelled the sickly-sweet rot before she saw it. Tendrils spiraled across the floor and up the walls. They originated from a plain wooden trunk in the far corner. Dark splotches marred the floor around it. At first she thought they were drips of rot, but they were red, not black.

The trunk was closed but not locked. She opened it. Inside was a wooden handle, smooth from repeated gripping. Long strips of leather ending in sharp metal barbs hung from the other end. The barbs were covered in blood that was already starting to dry to a dark, rusty orange shade. The bottom of the trunk was stained the same color.

She'd seen a similar device in a horror movie once. The movie had centered around a satanic cult. Cult members walked around holding the handle in both hands and swinging the device back and forth so that the barbs bit into the skin of their backs.

She thought of the red on Dimmesdale's white shirt and shivered. Some religious people practiced self-flagellation, right? Maybe this wasn't as weird as it seemed... but he'd been awfully quick to hide what he was doing.

She decided it didn't matter and focused her attention on the ink rot. It was worse than what had happened to the small boy. Dimmesdale was lucky it hadn't spread to him yet.

Dorian had told her to wait until he came back if the rot was extensive, but if she did, she was sure he'd keep her from doing anything. He'd say it was too dangerous, that she needed to rest and gain strength.

But she couldn't do that. Dimmesdale had been right. She couldn't even begin to make up for Andre's death if she did the same things she would have done otherwise. She had to do more, sacrifice more, risk more.

And if you fail... well, that will be a form of penance, won't it?

She reached out and touched the rot, and it moved up her arm like it had the previous night. She was surprised to find it almost sentient. Aware. It knew she wanted to destroy it, and it began to pulsate.

Sentient had been the wrong word. It wasn't sentient. It was more like a virus, a thing that consumes not because of need or desire but simply because that's what it does. It didn't care about the destruction or pain it caused. It didn't even care to protect itself. It reminded her of the way the UNCs—the unnamed characters—protected the gate indiscriminately when it was threat-ened. She knew, somehow, that the two things were related.

It advanced up her arm, stopping an inch from her elbow. It contracted slightly, and she felt pressure on her arm, and then a sudden wave of exhaustion overcame her. It swelled and contracted again.

It was feeding off her like a leech. Sucking away her energy and lifeforce. Was this what its victims felt?

"April!"

Dorian's voice came from behind her, and then he was at her side. She could barely keep her eyes open to look at him.

"Damn it, woman," he said. "I told you to wait for me!"

"Don't yell at me," she said sleepily. It would be nice to sleep, now...

"April?" Panic rose in his voice. "You have to fight it!"

"Can't." The one-word response was all she could manage.

"You can," Dorian said. "You have to. Mae was able to do this like it was nothing, so it's not impossible. You have to try."

She tried to respond to him, to tell him how the fatigue had settled into her bones, but the words didn't come out.

"You have to try," Dorian said. "Otherwise what's happening to you now will happen to everyone else here. And it doesn't end with this, April. You'll still exist, but you'll only be a shell of yourself."

She tried to listen to what he was saying, but he seemed to be drifting away. It was like he was speaking to her over a bad telephone connection.

"If you give up now, all of this would have been for nothing! Andre would have died for nothing!"

Her eyes shot open. *No.* She thought of finding Andre. She had felt so an-gry at herself. She found that anger again and turned it outward towards the rot. She would not let it win, no matter how much it hurt.

The rot hissed and pulled away. Its edges curled up like a slug touching salt, but it was her turn to not let it go. It tried to pull away, but she held fast, feeling it dry out, watching as flakes of it blew into the air.

Then the whole tendril of rot turned to dust and dispersed in a cloud of powder.

She fell backwards, Dorian catching her.

"Are you okay?"

"I think so," she said. She felt as tired as if she'd run a marathon, but it wasn't the soul-sucking weariness that she'd felt when the rot had her in its clutches. "It's alive," she tried to explain. "But not really. It just consumes and destroys."

"Shh," Dorian said. "Tell me about it later. Save your strength."

"April!" Randall was in the room. "What happened?"

"What happened is that April doesn't know how to follow directions." Then his voice softened. "She's exhausted. We need to get her back to the library. Maybe Barty can whip something up to return a little of her energy."

They gripped her elbows and led her back out into the church's main room, where Arthur Dimmesdale had re-entered just in time to see them emerging from the anteroom.

"Have thou entered my private chamber?" He asked, the color draining from his face.

"I'm sorry, Reverend," Dorian said smoothly. "Our cousin is not well. She's prone to fits as of late. She blames herself for an accident that took place in our home town."

April couldn't tell if the Reverend believed the excuse because Dorian and Randall whisked her away before he could react. She allowed them to half-carry her back to the gate. She was too tired to do anything else.

Once back in the library they deposited her on the couch in the sitting area. Randall and Barty went down to the break room to make tea. Dorian remained behind.

He spoke, and his voice was low and intense, almost angry. "I'm all for getting the ink rot under control—it was my idea from the beginning, if you remember—but killing yourself wasn't what I had in mind."

"I'm fine."

"You certainly aren't."

"I don't want anyone else to get hurt because of me."

"What about the people in the books? If you overestimate your abilities again, what will happen to them?"

"They'll be fine," she said.

Dorian let out an exasperated breath. "How, if you're not here to clean up the ink rot?"

"You'll find someone else to replace me," she said.

There were several beats of silence, then he said, "Is that what you think? That you're replaceable?"

"Well, yes."

Barty and Randall walked back into the room before he could answer. A steaming cup of tea was thrust into April's hands. She took a sip, not paying attention to its contents.

She almost spit it out but forced herself to swallow. The scalding liquid, though nearly odorless, was almost unbearably bitter. The closest taste she had reference for was ear wax.

Her gag reflex protested, but she managed to keep it down. "This is awful. It's tea?"

"It's whatever was in the Tupperware container in the cupboard. I cast a small energy-replenishing charm on it. Got me through many a cram session at college," Barty said, grinning. "The magic causes the bitter taste. I can't figure out how to get rid of it."

"Huh," April said, examining the mug. She felt like she'd chugged an energy drink, but without the jittery side effects.

"You'll want to drink the rest of it before it cools down," Barty said apologetically. "It's even worse cold."

She pinched her nose and poured the rest of the bitter liquid down her throat before her taste buds could react. When she'd finished it, the corners of her mouth pulled out into a grimace.

She set the mug down. Despite the aftertaste lingering in her mouth, she felt better than she had all day.

She stood. "Okay. What's the next book?"

"Are you mad?" Dorian said, "You nearly fainted! What would have happened if I hadn't arrived in time?"

For a split second, April's mind flashed to the moments where she had almost given in to the rot. If Dorian knew how close she'd been...

"It would have been fine." That's all she'd been doing since she came back to work, telling people that she was fine.

"Bloody hell it would have."

Randall and Dorian stood between her and the gate. She addressed Dorian. "Look. You're the one who's always saying the rot's gotten out of control. So what's the problem?"

"What will you do if the same thing happens again?" Dorian asked.

"Barty can make more of that awful tea."

"Actually," Barty said, "I can't. If you take too much in a short period of time you'll get addicted."

"I thought this was magic, not a drug."

"It's no more a drug than coffee. It just loses its effectiveness until you need impossibly large quantities for the same effect."

"Okay. We'll do a book where the ink rot is more manageable." She crossed her arms. "I'm doing this, so if you guys want to stop me you better be ready to take me down."

Dorian pressed his palm to his temple. "One book," he said finally, "*Of my choice*, and no tomfoolery this time."

"Of course," she said.

With a sigh, he went over to the bookshelf and rifled through the volumes.

Chapter Four

April's dreams that night started in Dimmesdale's church, and ended with smoldering fire and hot coal against skin. The heat had soothed her muscles, sore even in her dreams...

When she finally opened her eyes, the unexpected brightness made her sit up in bed. She'd overslept again. She checked her phone—nearly noon. Gram would kill her.

She scrambled out of bed and padded out into the living room. She still wore her clothes from the previous evening.

Gram was in the kitchen. April steeled herself for her harsh admonishment for sleeping so late. Gram leaned over the kitchen table, scribbling. April thought she was working on a crossword puzzle, but she was writing something on a piece of lined notebook paper.

"Hey, Gram."

"Oh, hey, April." Gram flipped the notebook paper over when she saw her. "You slept late. You're not still sick, are you?" Gram's hand stayed firmly on the back of the paper.

"I'm fine, Gram," April said. "I went out with some co-workers last night and I guess I overdid it. I didn't even hear my alarm go off." She didn't mention that she'd never set it.

"Oh," Gram said. "It's good you're making work friends. You don't go out often enough. Just don't make it a habit." Gram tapped her fingers impatiently on the table and glanced down at the paper in front of her. What was she up to?

Gram squinted down at April's chest. "What is that?" she said.

April looked down. Barty's amulet had slipped out over the neck of her t-shirt. April tucked it back in. "One of the kids made it at a craft program and gave it to me. I forgot to take it off." Trying to steer the conversation away from the amulet, she asked, "What are you writing?"

"Nothing. A letter."

"Does it have something to do with your diagnosis?"

"No." Gram touched her neck, a sure sign that she was lying. Gram was a terrible liar.

April shook her head. What could be so bad that Gram wouldn't want to share it with her? "If you're trying to protect me from something, don't. I'll just worry more wondering what it is."

Gram sighed. "There's nothing to worry about. I was going to keep it a secret. I mean, it probably won't even happen..."

"What won't happen?"

"Well... you know that trip we always talked about taking when you were in high school?" Gram asked, her voice hopeful, almost girlish.

There was only one trip they'd ever really talked about taking. "The one across Europe? Yeah. But we could never afford it. That was just wishful talk."

"I know, but... you've heard about the Make A Wish Foundation, right?"

April nodded. "Yeah, they grant wishes for kids."

Gram nodded. "There's a similar foundation called Senior Star that provides the same service to seniors. One of my friends from spin class told me about it. Her sister had emphysema and she wrote them a letter, and they sent her and her husband on a cruise."

"Oh."

"I feel a little selfish even applying. if I get picked, does that mean some other poor person gets denied? But... we could take the trip we always wanted to take." She paused hopefully. "So, what do you think?"

"Oh, Gram," April said. If Gram had told her this three weeks ago, April would have told her to mail the letter. She probably wouldn't get selected, but there was no harm in applying. But what if she *was* chosen? A trip to Europe would take at least a week, maybe longer. April couldn't be away from the library for so much time, not with the ink rot looming over her head.

"You think it's stupid," Gram said. The light that had been in her eyes extinguished. "You're right. Why get my hopes up?"

"Gram, that's not what I meant."

"Of course not." Gram looked away. "I have to get ready for yoga. I promised Ethel I'd go with her today."

She walked down the hall, and April felt too exhausted to stop her. Maybe Dorian was right, maybe she had taken on too much the night before.

~~~

They spent each night of the following week attacking the ink rot. Dorian watched her closely, making sure not to leave her alone. There weren't any more close calls, but April went home exhausted every night, feeling like she'd been physically beaten, and each morning her muscles were as sore as if she'd been lifting weights. But it was never enough; every night she dreamed of Andre, and each dream ended in burning fire.

At the end of the night the following Monday, April sent Barty and Randall home. Barty had given Randall a ride, and as soon as the illuminated delivery topper on Barty's beat-up sedan disappeared down the street, April walked back to the shelf that housed the Werner books.

"What are you doing?" Dorian said as he crossed his arms.

"This isn't for work." April lifted the book cover so he could see it. *One Thousand and One Nights.*

"Why would you go back there?" Dorian said.

"I want to visit an old friend."

"The djinni?" A look of understanding came over Dorian's face. His lip curled.

April's face flushed. "I never thanked him."

"He owed you a favor. Anyway, didn't he threaten to leave you in the desert? What if he does something like that again?"

"He won't." At least she didn't think he would.

"Well, I'm not going in with you."

"I don't recall inviting you." She thought of the genie's burning kiss. "You'd probably be uncomfortable, anyway."

Dorian's face darkened even further. "I see."

"Look, I need this, okay? It's been a hard couple of weeks."

"You can do what you like. You're a grown woman."

"And you're not my father."

"Fine. Just be careful, and don't come running to me when you get hurt." He turned away and walked to Mae's office, slamming the door behind him.

She looked down at the watch on her wrist. A little after two. She should be back by four-thirty. With time moving faster in *One Thousand and One Nights* than in the library, it shouldn't be an issue. Still, she shouldn't lose track of time. She opened the book to around the same place as last time but didn't bother to make sure it was exact. The genie would find her.

She waited for the gate to open and then stepped through it. She'd been in so many different landscapes and worlds that the dusty town felt comfortingly familiar. Almost.

She looked around her. "Genie!" she called.

"I have a name, you know."

She turned, and, as she did, she was no longer standing in the city street where she'd been moments before. She was inside a stone structure lit with torches and oil lamps. The room was draped in lush fabrics and silk cushions covered the floor. Sitting on one of the cushions was the genie. Two beautiful women sat at his feet—two scantily-clad women. A third sat in his lap with her arms draped around his shoulders.

"Hello, Sorceress," the genie said.

"I have a name, too." She looked down at the women with distaste. "Why did you bring me here?" she asked, though she already knew the answer. He wanted her to see him with these women.

"Why, Sorceress. You seem to think that I mean some offense. This is merely my place of business."

"You work in a... brothel?" she asked, her nose wrinkling.

"I *own* a brothel. Considering the restrictions you placed on me, I had to find a means to support myself that didn't involve hurting others. I am now in the boon business. A freelancer, you could say. One of my customers made enemies of the wrong people. He traded this establishment for my assistance."

April gestured to the women. "I suppose *this* is a benefit of owning a whorehouse?"

The genie's eyes flashed. "I do not pay for sex."

One of the women at his feet spoke. "This homely girl has insulted you. One word and I will pluck out her eyes."

"Oh, *please*," April said. "I have dealt with scarier things than you in the last few weeks."

The genie smiled. "Though the idea of the two of you fighting over me is intriguing... I think we will pass. I see it makes you uncomfortable." He looked down at the women. "Ladies, leave us."

Reluctantly, the women stood and walked away, shooting daggers at April with their eyes. April resisted the urge to stick her tongue out at the one who had threatened to kill her.

"Do you have them enchanted or something? Sex slaves?" Ick.

"I said I don't pay for sex. I should elaborate and say also that I only sleep with those who want to sleep with me. There's no fascination for me in force. Anyway, I believe enchanting them against their wills would break your restriction."

April raised a skeptical eyebrow. "They were all over you."

"Do you find it so hard to believe?"

She did not, so she chose to say nothing rather than stroke his already enflamed ego.

"The truth is, the man who owned this establishment before me deserved every bad thing coming his way. He treated these women like dogs—most of them kidnapped or purchased as children, beaten and intimidated for even the slightest infractions. He was a man who enjoyed force... and attracted clientele with similar tastes."

"So these women are lucky that you're their master now and not him?"

His eyes flamed once more. "I am no one's master. These women are free to come and go as they wish. They wept with joy when I first walked in here. Life on the street as a prostitute is as good as a death sentence." He paused. "It doesn't hurt that I am a generous and skilled lover."

She snorted.

"Jealous?"

"No. I could care less what you do." It was true. She really didn't care. She hadn't come there for a relationship.

Still, the genie smiled as though she were lying. "Why did you come?"

She crossed her arms. "Why do you keep coming into my dreams?"

His smile grew even wider. "So you're dreaming about me."

Her cheeks colored. "Only because you're doing something to make me dream about you," she said, then faltered. "Right?"

He laughed. "No. Intriguing as the thought is of entering your dreams is, the wall between your world and mine is impenetrable. I cannot cross over, even in the dreamworld."

He rose and began walking towards her, lithe as a tiger, then too quickly he was behind her, his breathe tickling her ear. "Which leaves me to wonder, why is a strange foreign sorceress dreaming of me?"

His breath raised goose flesh on the skin of her neck. It was like sitting close to a fire on a cold night when a sudden wind sends a wave of heat towards you.

"I... I have been stressed lately... dealing with the gate..."

"Hmm..." he breathed in, inhaling her scent. "I can sense the truth of that. But is that the real reason you came here?" His lips touched her skin.

"No," she gasped.

"Also true," he said, the words tickling her skin. He pulled the tail of her shirt from her skirt, then his hands were on her bare flesh, searing her. It was partially pleasant, partially painful... though mostly pleasant.

His hands pushed up her bra, brushing against her nipples before moving down towards the waistband of her skirt. Her breath caught in her throat.

"I do not force anyone," he said. "You want this, don't you?"

"Yes," she said. She licked her lips. They were dry, chapped.

"Do you believe that I am enchanting you, or otherwise impairing your judgement?"

"No."

"Good." His hands descended over her skin.

~~~

"I still don't know your name," April said. She lay with her head resting in his navel.

"Why?" He lay with his arms behind his head, staring up at the ceiling. "You're not falling in love with me, are you?"

"No way. This is the equivalent of an inter-world booty call."

"Booty call?"

"Sex, no strings attached." She wondered if he would understand the expression, so she added, "no emotions, no commitments."

He shifted and ran the tips of his fingers along her shoulderblades, making her shiver. "Hmm. I like no commitments. But sex without emotion seems pointless. It wasn't emotionless for you." He did not phrase this as a question, and because she didn't want to get into it any more than she already had, she didn't respond.

After a few minutes he spoke again. "Was it what you dreamed of?"

She shrugged, remembering how all of her dreams the previous week had ended in fire. "I thought it would burn more."

He smirked. "So it is fire you seek. But for destruction or purification?"

She looked at him. "Which do you offer?" She reached out to touch him, but he grabbed her wrist. It felt like being branded with hot iron.

"Hey," she said, and tried to pull her hand away, but he held fast.

"Is there a difference?" he held on a moment longer before releasing her. She ran her fingers over her skin expecting a blister in the shape of his fingers, but her skin was pale and blemish free.

"That was mean," she said. "And I thought you couldn't hurt anyone!"

"I didn't hurt you. It was all in your head."

He was right about that. The searing pain had already faded so that she couldn't remember it at all except for the fact that it existed.

"It was still mean!"

"You needed to feel the danger," he said. "I will be your lover but you need to leave your problems outside these walls."

"Fine." She was about to get up and put her clothes on, but then a familiar voice from the doorway made her blood run cold.

"April! What in god's name—"

"Dorian!" April pulled one of the silks over herself. "What are you doing here?"

"Looking for you," he said. His face was red and splotchy. "Do you have any idea what time it is?"

She winced. She hadn't looked at the timepiece since she'd arrived. Damn it. It couldn't be *that* late, though. "It is..." she looked surreptitiously at the watch. "Four forty-five." Crap. Had time really gone that fast?

"Turn around so I can get dressed," she said.

"Sorceress," the genie said. "Is this *boy* bothering you?" he smiled tauntingly at Dorian and rose without covering himself. It made the whole situation more awkward, if it was possible.

"Me bothering her? You're the one taking advantage of her!"

"Taking advantage? She came to me."

April shot the genie a hard look. "Leave him alone. I need to go."

The genie shrugged. "As you wish. I'm here, *whenever* you need me." He cupped her face in his hands and pressed his lips against hers. She got the feeling the kiss was more for Dorian's benefit than hers.

The genie walked out through the door the women had used earlier, leaving her alone with Dorian.

"Well, turn around," she said.

He did, crossing his arms over his chest. She pulled on her clothes. After a few minutes of excruciating silence she said, "Well, aren't you going to yell at me?"

"You know I never had to chase Mae around strange cities, finding her in the arms of degenerates! You know I had to ask around about your *friend* to try and figure out where you were? Can you imagine my embarrassment when they said he was the owner of a brothel!"

She rolled her eyes at his diatribe, but it was better than the judgmental quiet.

After she was dressed, they walked into the street. Dorian seemed to know the way back to the gate, so she followed him. "What do you see in that preening peacock anyway?"

"Peacock?" she asked, raising an eyebrow.

"You see how he's always *adjusting himself*"—he said this word with a look on his face that suggested he'd just tasted something sour—"and walking around without trousers on..."

No. It couldn't be... could it? "Are you... jealous of him?"

"Of course I'm not jealous!"

She stopped walking. "Oh, my goodness," she said, stopping herself from laughing. "Angel-faced Dorian Gray is jealous!"

"I said I wasn't jealous."

"Jeez, I'm sorry—"

"Please just... don't."

She fell into silence. She hadn't realized how much he disliked the genie. He sulked all the way back to the gate. He barely acknowledged her when she said goodnight.

Chapter Five

Gram was meeting a friend for lunch, so April only saw her for a few minutes. Again, she didn't comment on April's sleeping so late except to ask if she was feeling all right.

After Gram left, April thought about going back to bed, but decided to eat instead. As she pulled out the ingredients to make a peanut butter and banana sandwich, she noticed the letter Gram had been writing the previous day. It sat on top of Gram's recycling pile, which she meant to recycle every week but usually forgot about.

April picked up the letter. Underneath it was an application form and an envelope addressed in Gram's no-nonsense cursive. The paper was filled entirely on the front and half on the back.

I feel silly writing this letter to you. There are so many people who have it worse than me. So far I'm living pain free. It feels selfish to ask for this, to take this opportunity away from someone who really needs it, maybe someone who hasn't had as many blessings in life as I have.

April snorted. That was Gram for you. Not only had she fought cancer—twice—but she'd lost her only son and daughter-in-law to an automobile accident. She hadn't been exactly wealthy, either. She and Grandpa had worked longer than most people had to, scrimping away their tiny savings that had been obliterated in a matter of months when Gram's insurance refused to cover her treatment. Only Gram would still say she was "blessed."

It's because of one of those blessings that I decided to write this after all. My granddaughter, April, lives with me. Her parents died when she was a child. When I was diagnosed with cancer, she quit school to come home and care for me.

Maybe I should have led with the cancer part. I was diagnosed with breast cancer two years ago. I beat it the first time, but now the doctors say it's reoccurred and has "metastasized." There's nothing they can do. Isn't that the pits?

Beating cancer wasn't cheap. I had a small amount of savings to leave to April when I died, but the insurance company refused to pay my bills so that's gone. What did April do? She got a job, and slowly she's getting us out of debt.

Despite all the world has thrown at her, April has remained hardworking and positive.

Now, I have nothing left to leave her except the house we live in, and that isn't much. But if I could, I'd love to leave her one last memory. We've always spoken about going to Europe—Paris, Rome, someplace in the Alps. Really, we're not picky. The most important thing is that it's a shared experience.

So that's my wish. I would love to be able to take my granddaughter on one trip together. She deserves it.

April's vision blurred before she could read Gram's signature at the bottom. Gram shouldn't be worrying about her... but it was so much like her to do so. Of course, April didn't deserve a trip to Europe, not after what she'd done... but she'd die before she let Gram know that.

April picked up the envelope and the entry form, both of which Gram had already filled out.

What the hell. She folded the letter and the entry form into thirds and slipped them into the envelope and started searching for a stamp. She'd slip it into the outgoing mail at work.

~~~

April sat at the reference desk, Randall sat in a nearby armchair. They'd spent a week with their intensive regime against the ink rot, and while she was tired, she no longer woke up in the morning feeling like she'd been in a street fight the night before. Dorian was right, she *had* gotten stronger.

She would have to thank him—and apologize. He'd been right. Taking it slower than she would have liked made her more effective, and now she could help more people. Not that she planned to slow down. She'd keep pushing herself, improving until she could restore the black books.

She gazed at the students studying at the tables and felt... peaceful. Not the same as before, but like she could live with the way things were, with what had happened to Andre.

The phone rang. "Third floor reference."

"Hello again, Ms. Walker."

She sighed. "Thaddeus, I really don't have time for this right now. Can't you just leave me alone?"

There was a pause on the other end of the line. "I guess you've taken time to consider my offer, then."

"I have," she said, though she hadn't had much of a chance to think about it.

"And?"

She thought. This could be her ticket out of all this, couldn't it? She could turn her back on the Werner Room, on the gate, on all of it. Then she wouldn't have to be the one making all the decisions.

But then she thought of the boy in the meadow, of Arthur Dimmesdale, and all the other people she had saved. Who would protect them?

"No," she said, and it was possibly the hardest syllable she'd ever had to say. "My answer is still no."

"I see. That is regrettable." Pause. "Goodbye, Ms. Walker."

Her hand shook as she replaced the phone on its cradle.

Randall looked up at her and smiled at the look on her face. She smiled back. She returned to her computer work.

"Hello?"

She looked up from her computer to see the source of the voice. Rico, Andre's son, stood in front of the desk.

"Rico," she said. "What are you doing here?"

Rico shrugged. "I'm here to pick up my dad's stuff."

"Oh, right. Becky has it." She picked up the walkie talkie, surprised by how damp her palms were. "Becky? Andre's son is here to pick up his things."

"I didn't even see him walk by," Becky said. "I'll bring the box upstairs. I could use a vacation from the children's desk."

April stifled a groan. She'd hoped she could send him downstairs. She didn't like the way he was looking at her. She placed the walkie talkie back in its cradle.

She looked at Rico and tried to smile. "Where's your mom?"

"At home."

"She sent you here to pick up your dad's things?"

He shrugged. "She said it wasn't worth the effort to pick them up. I came here by myself."

"Oh."

April tried to return to the spreadsheet she'd been working on, but her vision kept going out of focus. She wondered what was taking Becky so long.

"Is that *The First Adventure of Braddy Evers?*" Rico asked, pointing to the pedestal.

"Yes," April said, relieved to have something to talk about. "It's a first edition copy."

"What's that mean?"

"It means this was one of the first copies ever printed. Are you a Braddy Evers fan?"

He nodded and licked his lips. "Dad used to read it to me when I was little."

"Oh," she said, and because she couldn't think of anything else, "You should come back on Braddy Evers Day. It's going to be lots of fun."

"Yeah, maybe," Rico said, but he didn't seem interested. "Ms. Walker... Can I ask you a question?"

She winced. His tone of voice indicated he wasn't going to ask for more info on Braddy Evers Day. "Of course."

"Do you know where my dad is?"

Time seemed to freeze for a second. Of all the things that Rico might have asked her, this seemed to be the worst possibility. Did he know something? How could he? She tried to keep her face neutral. "No, hon. Why would you think I do?"

Rico looked disappointed. "I don't know. You looked scared the first time you saw me, and you were gone the week after he went missing." He paused, then said earnestly, "I won't tell my mom where he is. I just want to ask him why he left."

"Oh, hon," April said. Her tear ducts started to burn. "I... I really don't know where your dad is. I'm sorry." She tried to tell herself it was technically true, and that the lie was a necessary one. But saving the lives of every person in the Werner collection couldn't be worth this.

"Oh," Rico said. He looked down at his shoes.

Becky walked into the room. "Hi, Rico," she said. "How are you doing?"

With one last look in April's direction Rico walked towards Becky. He took the box from her, and she patted him on the shoulder and said a few words that April couldn't hear before heading back downstairs.

She willed him to leave, instead, he dug through the box. He paused at the picture of himself before pulling out the jacket Andre kept at work. After a few seconds of staring at it, he pulled it on, and then left.

April rose and walked quickly to her office and closed the door behind her. She felt like crying but her eyes remained dry. In her mind's eye she kept seeing Rico holding his father's jacket.

When she looked up Randall was there, which was weird because she didn't remember the door opening.

"Hey," he said, using the same voice he had when he'd come over to her house the previous week. "You okay? You ran in here pretty fast."

"Does someone have a reference question?" she asked.

He shook his head. "No. I just saw you talking to the boy. He's Andre's son, isn't he?"

She didn't answer, and he shifted uneasily back and forth on his feet. Rex whined.

"That kid is never going to know what happened to his father," April said. "He's going to grow up thinking Andre abandoned him. And he's always going to wonder why."

"I know."

"So what do I do?" She held her breath, hoping that Randall would have an answer, because she sure as hell didn't.

"Just what you're doing now," Randall said. "Your best."

"If this is my best, then we're screwed." She nodded towards the door. "We better go back out. People will start wondering..." she'd been about to say that they would start wondering if she'd gone missing, but then she realized what that sounded like and fought back the words. "they might start wondering where I am. Let's go."

~~~

April stepped out of Mae's office that night after close to find Dorian, Randall, and Barty with their heads almost pressed together speaking in low voices. They stopped talking as soon as they saw her.

"What's going on?" She said, crossing her arms.

They exchanged a worried glance. Dorian was the first to speak. "We've been discussing it, and we think you should take some time off."

"Discussing it?" She said. "You mean planning a mutany!"

"You need time to heal," Randall said. "You've been pushing yourself too hard."

"What?" she said. "I've barely been breaking a sweat the last few nights. It was hard at first, but I'm getting stronger, just like Dorian said."

"I don't mean physically," Randall said. "After that boy came in today you were obviously not okay."

"That boy is Andre's son," April said.

"I know that."

"If I take a break, who's going to maintain the collection, huh?"

"You've been working at a break-neck pace," Dorian said. "An extended weekend isn't going to harm anything."

"I'll lose the muscle I've built!" April said. "I need to keep increasing my abilities, or else I'll never be able to fix the black books!"

There was a long beat of silence.

"I told you," Dorian said, "there's nothing you can do for the black books."

"I have to at least try," she said. She tried to make eye contact with each of them. "Randall? Back me up, here."

"You need to take care of yourself before you can take care of anyone else," he said.

"Barty?"

Barty looked down at his feet and said nothing.

"Fine. That's just fine. If you guys aren't going to help me, you can just leave."

"April—"

"Just go."

All that could be heard in the following silence was the ticking of the grandfather clock. Barty was the one to break it. "Let's go, Randall. I'll give you a ride."

Their steps echoed all the way down the stairwell. When the downstairs door had shut, April turned to Dorian. "You, too."

"That's fine," Dorian said. "You don't know which books have the ink rot."

He was right. She ground her teeth. "Whateverqu. I'll figure it out myself."

Without another word, Dorian walked to the place near the gate where the copy of his book was hidden. He pulled it out from under the floorboards and opened it. As the gate opened, he said, "This is for the best. You don't see it now, but you will. Just a few days."

She closed the book on him, turning away so she wouldn't have to see his disappointed expression.

She'd thought that kicking them out might make her feel better, but she only felt more agitated. Dorian was right; she didn't know which books had ink rot and which didn't. She could go through them randomly, but that was a waste of effort...

But it wasn't qiute true, was it? She knew where *some* of the ink rotted books were.

She went to Mae's office, testing the floorboards until she found a a loose section underneath her desk. She pulled it up and there they were, about a dozen of them, each cover so black it was indistinguishable from its neighbor. She shivered at the thought of sitting above them while she worked.

She pulled one out and walked out to the gate and opened it. Once the gate was opened, what lay beyond was exactly the same as what she had seen in the black book the previous week. Dark shapes of varying sizes, some that must have been buildings and others that could have been automobiles, and faceless, shadowy figures.

She stood in front of the gate for a long while. Was she going in? No, she finally decided. Dorian was right. She wasn't strong enough yet. But she would be, someday.

She sat on the nearest table and watched the blackened masses move and shift on the other side.

"Ms. Walker?"

April's head snapped towards the double doors where the noise had come from. There shouldn't be anyone in the library. The library seemed dim after staring at the light-sucking ink rot; she had to narrow her eyes to make out the figure standing on the other side of the veil. It was Rico.

Chapter Six

She slammed the book shut, but it was too late. He had already seen. Once the gate was closed, she turned to Rico. "What are you doing here? How did you get in?"

He ignored her question, looking instead at the stained-glass window. "What was all that?"

She raised her eyebrow at him. "I asked you first."

He shrugged. "I found some keys in my dad's jacket."

He reached into the jacket pocket and pulled out a set of keys identical to April's. Andre must have had a spare set.

"That explains *how* you got in, but it doesn't explain why."

Rico looked down at his feet. "I dunno. I guess I thought my dad might be here." He scuffed the toe of his sneaker against the hardwood floor.

April's face softened. She wanted to tell him his father would never leave him, that he'd be here if he could. But that was the same thing as telling him his dad was dead. She couldn't bring herself to utter the words. What would be worse, thinking your dad abandoned you, or knowing he was dead? She couldn't make that decision.

"Why would you think he was here?" It was a deflection, and she hated herself for being so weak.

Rico looked uncomfortable again. "My mom thinks you're sleeping with my dad," his face turned a bright shade of purple. "I was walking down the street and saw the light on, and, I don't know... I thought he might be here."

"Your dad and I weren't—aren't—involved," she said, not able to make herself say *sleeping with* to a twelve year old.

"Oh. Well, my mom says a lot of things." He looked down at his feet again before looking at the gate. "What was that? Some kind of video?"

"Uh, yeah," she said. It was as good an answer as any.

"It looks like just a regular window," he said skeptically.

"You know, you really aren't supposed to be here," she said. "I'm going to call your mom and have her come pick you up."

Rico backed away from her. "That's okay... I'll just walk home."

She placed her hand on her hip. "I can't just let you leave. You broke into the library. I should be calling the cops."

Rico hung his head. "Fine," he said glumly.

"You stay here," she said, and hurried back to Mae's office. She made sure to take the black book with her—the last thing she needed was for Rico to open it while she was gone.

She had to boot up Mae's computer to find the employee contact list. Hopefull Rico's mom was at Andre's apartment and not somewhere else... after searching for what felt like forever, she finally found the contact list and wrote down the number. She hurried back out—she'd call from the phone on the reference desk so she could keep an eye on Rico.

But when she walked out past the book shelves, the gate was open.

Her heart suddenly pumped a million miles an hour. "Rico?" she called. She'd never be able to explain Rico seeing the gate to Dorian. There was a book open on the table. She lifted it so she could read the title, careful not to lose the page. *The First Adventure of Braddy Evers.*

He must have taken the book down off the stand on her desk to look at it while she waited. Why had she left him out there by himself? She just assumed that everyone was like her and wouldn't pick up a book unless they absolutely had to.

"Rico?" she called, hoping he was in the library still. There was no answer. He couldn't have left through the double-doors; she would have seen him through the office window.

Growing more and more frantic, she checked the vault and the restrooms. Nothing.

Finally she had to accept what she'd dreaded since she saw the open gate: Rico had gone into the pages of *The First Adventure of Braddy Evers.*

Chapter Seven

April debated over whether she should try to collect Dorian, Barty, and Randall before going to look for Rico, but if she did, that gave Rico even more time to stumble away from the gate.

She glanced through the veil. The scene on the other side was dense, bright green forest. There was no sign of Rico. She'd have to go in and look for him.

The air on the otherside of the veil was cool, and the forest's undergrowth was spongey beneath her shoes. The sky through the trees above was just beginning to darken. The gate had opened in a door set into a small hill. Judging by the smell of sour grapes, it was used to store wine.

"Rico?" she called. No response.

A small trail worn into the forest led away from the cellar. It looked like the best bet for finding Rico, so she followed it. As she did, she could hear voices, and music. The trees quickly thinned, revealing an outdoor dining area filled with long mess-hall style tables. Sitting at the tables or chatting around a well-laden buffet were dozens of squat children.

A band of musicians holding instruments that almost resembled acoustic guitars and flutes played from a wooden stage. The area was lined with tall torches stuck into the ground. Two dirt paths on either side of the dining area were also lined with torches.

"Ms. Walker!"

April turned towards the sound of her name, and relief flooded her body as she saw Rico. He waved her over enthusiastically.

She didn't know what she'd been expecting, but it wasn't for him to be sitting at one of the tables with a giant plate of food in front of him.

She ran over. "Thank goodness you're all right."

He grinned widely. "Can you believe this? When I saw the window open I thought the television or projector or whatever had turned on somehow, but then I saw that I could walk through it! I'm in Groundsville! This is amazing!"

"Groundsville?" she asked.

"You know—Braddy Evers hometown? Where all the groundlings live?"

She shook her head. "I've never read this book."

His mouth fell open. "You've never read *The First Adventure of Braddy Evers?*"

She shook her head.

"But you're a *librarian!*"

"Why is everyone always saying that?" She put her hands on her hips. "You're okay with walking into a book world, but not with the fact that I haven't read every book on the planet?"

Rico shrugged.

"We need to go back, now. Your mother will be worried sick."

Rico shrugged. "No she won't. She doesn't care about me at all."

"That's not true," April said, but didn't know what else to say to make the words sound genuine.

"Can't we just stay for a little while longer? Labhras is about to put on the magic show!"

She was going to insist they head back, but the look on his face changed her mind. His dad was dead because of her. The least she could give him was an hour of happiness.

"Fine," she said, and slid into the seat across from him.

"Yes!" he said, forming his hand into a fist and pulling his arm back by the elbow emphatically. He reached for a cup of maroon liquid, but she grabbed it away from him.

"I think you've had enough," she said. She was about to toss it out, but it smelled sweet, so she took a draw.

"That's not fair," he started, but she raised an eyebrow at him and he fell silent.

"How long have you been here, anyway?"

"A few hours at least," he said.

"*A few hours?* And what have you been doing that whole time?"

He shrugged. "I came through the gate, and this groundling woman started yelling at me to help carry casks of wine to the party. So I did. Then she told me to do some other stuff—bringing out the food and all that. I've been sitting down for maybe fifteen minutes."

"So what's with all the kids?" April asked.

Rico's voice got low. "They're not kids. They're groundlings. They live underneath the roots of trees."

April looked at the nearest groundlings, a man and woman who were seated at the same table as she and Rico. Their faces were lined, and the man had a beard. Definitely not children.

"Eat up, Marn," the woman said. "You're getting too thin these days. We don't want the hosts to think we don't like their food, do we?"

There were four plates stacked in front of Marn, and he was working on a fifth. He grunted and kept eating, his pace unaffected.

"Groundlings eat a lot," Rico whispered to April.

"I see." April leaned over and spoke to the woman. "What are we celebrating?" she asked.

The woman eyed her suspiciously. "I think you need to slow down on yer wine, dear. It's three-twelfs day. Everyone knows that."

"You're right, I think I do need to slow down on the drinking," April said. "What is three-twelfs day?"

"It's three twelfs of the way through the summer. I 'spose next you'll be asking what's a-thirds day!"

"But there's only three months in the summer." April hoped that wherever they were, the seasons were the same. "That means there's a celebration like this every week?"

"Aye," the woman said, becoming quite serious. "Some people think it should be more often, but what with birthdays and deathdays and what not, there won't be enough days for all the celebratin.'"

Rico batted at her elbow, drawing her attention away from Marn and the woman. He pointed to a nearby clearing where a tall figure stood—more than twice as tall as any groundling they'd seen. "That's him," he said, the color draining from his face.

"Who?"

"*Labhras*—the magician!"

Though April had never read the books, she recognized the name. She focused more on the figure, and when she did, she made out the shape of a large top hat. In his hand was a long thin object that might have been a wand.

"Oh," she said. "Cool."

"*Cool?* It's more than cool. That's him! The magician!"

April suppressed a giggle. "Do you want to go talk to him?"

"No," he said. "No. I can't."

She shrugged. "Suit yourself." She watched the figure. "What's he doing, anyway?"

"He puts on magic shows for the groundlings' celebrations and festivals."

"That must be a good gig," April said, remembering what the woman had said about festivals, birthdays, and deathdays.

Rico nodded. "He's also the one that recruits Braddy to the adventure party."

The magic show was the best she'd ever seen. Labhras must have been practicing real magic, it was the only explanation for some of the feats he performed, including a puppet show where the characters were made up of colored lights.

April looked down at Rico, expecting to see him watching the display. Instead, his eyes were on a man sitting at the table across from them. He held his daughter—who was no more than three—on his shoulders so she could see better. Rico's smile was gone.

"You okay?" April asked.

He looked down at his empty plate. "My dad didn't leave, did he?"

Oh, no. April searched for words that could make the situation seem better. Why did it have to be her who decided what Rico knew and believed about the world?

But she couldn't lie. "No, he didn't."

"He's dead."

He waited for her to say something, but she couldn't find the words. To respond felt too final, too harsh.

"It was in a book, wasn't it?"

"Yes. Not this one. A different one."

"Was it that one you were looking into? The one that was all black?"

She shook her head. "No."

The magician's display ended in a finale of fireworks that exploded above their heads and brightened the sky, making Rico's face as visible as if it were high noon. His features were as hard as stone.

Then the blasts faded, leaving trails and clouds of smoke that slowly drifted down towards the ground.

"I'm never going to see him again."

"Rico..."

Before she could think of something to say—really, what words were there?—he rose from the table and ran off into the dark.

"Rico!" By the time she managed to stand he was gone. She ran after him, stopping in front of a building with the smell of baking bread wafting from it—the bakery. Rico had said he'd helped carry bread from a bakery. Inside, an older groundling woman was cleaning.

When she saw April, she yelled, "We're closed."

"The boy who was helping you carry bread earlier... have you seen him?"

The woman shrugged. "Run off, has he? Tryin' to shirk cleanup duty, no doubt."

"So you haven't seen him?" April said, her heart sinking.

"Can't say I have. But if you find him, tell him there's work to be done."

April ran back into the road. How was she going to find him?

She jogged down the road. Occasionally a partygoer would pass by, and she would ask if they had seen Rico. Those that weren't too inebriated replied that they hadn't.

Once she reached the other end of the village, which was outlined by a border of torches set on long sticks, she stopped. Rico was nowhere to be seen. She looked into the darkness of the forest beyond the edge of the torches' light. He wouldn't have gone in there, would he? He'd been pretty upset. People did dumb things when they were upset.

Wherever he was, she couldn't search for him alone. She needed help. She checked Mae's timepiece. A little after eleven.

She ran, following the line of torches back to the area where the party had been. Most of the guests had gone home. Those that remained were gathering up the dirty dishes and wiping down the long tables.

April slipped into the woods towards the wine cellar. She grabbed one of the torches as she passed, holding it out in front of her to light her way.

She found the gate easily despite the darkness, a stroke of luck in an otherwise terrible night.

April went to the reference desk and dialed the number for St. Mary's. The tired-sounding woman who answered said they didn't generally take messages for shelter guests, but she promised to relay the message to Randall after hearing the panic in April's voice. Then she called Barty's cell phone.

She sat down and waited. She knew she should get Dorian, but she was afraid to close the gate. What if Rico came back to the gate and it was closed?

After what felt like an eternity, Barty, Randall, and Rex burst into the Werner Room. Randall rushed over to her. "Are you okay?" he asked, his forehead creased.

"You got here fast," she said, unable to answer his question without breaking down.

"Barty picked us up."

Barty nodded. "They were running like the devil was chasing them." He removed his Nemo's ballcap. "Where's Dorian?"

Without speaking, she placed one of Dorian's index cards inside *The Groundling* to mark the page, then closed it. She opened *The Picture of Dorian Gray*.

Dorian was seated on the divan as the gate began to open, a surprised look on his face. By the time the gate opened he'd come to stand in front of it.

"What day is it?" he asked as he stepped through the veil. "An entire night hasn't passed, has it?"

"It's the same night," April said. She closed *The Picture of Dorian Gray* as soon as Dorian had passed through. She opened *The First Adventure of Braddy Evers,* her eyes scanning the forest behind Dorian. Rico wasn't there.

Dorian looked between her and the others. "What's going on?" he asked.

"We were wondering the same thing," Barty said.

She told them about Rico running away in *The First Adventure of Braddy Evers.*

"How did he get into the library?" Randall asked.

"He found Andre's keys."

"*And you decided the best thing to do next was to leave him alone in front of the gate*? With a roomful of books that could open it?" Dorian was rubbing his temples as though he had a headache.

"I... wasn't thinking clearly."

"That's for certain."

"You can rake me over the coals later. Right now, we need to find him before the gate shuts for the day." She pulled a blank piece of paper from the printer at the reference desk and began scribbling a simple map of the groundling village.

"The gate opens here. This is where the party was. This path leads through the village. I ran down that one, but didn't see him."

"That doesn't mean he isn't there now," Randall said.

"You're right. We'll check there again." She pointed to the path she'd seen on the other side of the outside dining area. "There's another path here that I haven't searched."

Randall nodded. "I've seen Rico around the library, but how will Dorian know what he looks like?"

Dorian spoke, his voice distant. "He'll be the one who's not a groundling."

"Oh, right."

April nodded. "Okay. I'll search here, you two search these areas"—she pointed to different sections of the map—"and we'll meet back at the party square at four forty-five at the latest."

Randall thought for a moment. "How will we know what time it is? You're the only one with a watch that works."

"Good point. Uh... here, I'll whistle like this"—she whistled three distinct notes—"at four thirty. That should give you time to get back to the gate."

Randall nodded. "And if we find him, we'll do the same."

April nodded. Either way, they'd be meeting back at the gate. She looked at Barty. "Can we count on you to watch over home base?"

Barty nodded. "Of course."

"Leave the gate open," April instructed. "He might find his way back. He's just a scared kid. He doesn't know how dangerous it can be."

Randall and Barty nodded. Dorian just continued to stare into the distance, his face blank and his arms crossed tightly over his chest.

"What about you, Dorian?"

Dorian didn't look at her. "I'll do what I have to do get the boy back safely and ensure the integrity of the gate."

She nodded. He didn't need to be happy, just committed. "Good."

They walked to the gate. To her surprise, Dorian spoke again as the gate was opening. "If we don't find the boy—"

"We'll find him," April said. They had to.

"But if we don't," Dorian continued, "We need to grab someone else to take his place here on this side once the gate becomes inactive for the day. The gate can't bear that much imbalance. It will shatter."

"So we should kidnap someone?"

"If we have to."

She didn't say anything else. She really hoped they didn't have to.

They crossed over. Time had passed more quickly in Groundsville than at the library. It was still night on the other side, though it was a deeper, darker night. The village was calm and still, and even the torches lining the path burned low, if they hadn't already sputtered out.

They separated. "Rico," April called. "Rico!" She didn't dare yell too loudly, lest she wake someone up. She searched the bakery and looked in the windows of all the nearby buildings. Nothing. She took one of the torches that still burned and started to walk. She'd seen a small path beyond the dining area. She followed it, calling Rico's name as she did.

The path led to what she sensed was a large open space. She raised the torch and it illuminated rows of plants. Farmlands. She continued to follow the path, calling Rico's name. Gigantic trees dotted the landscape, though it wasn't the forest that Groundsville was. Rico had said that groundlings lived under the roots of trees.

Taking a chance, she approached on of the trees. Sure enough, the massive roots, some as large around as her own waist, were above ground. A door and several windows was visible in the spaces between them.

She looked through one of the windows. Inside was a bedroom. The twin-sized bed was empty, the blankets rumpled and cast aside.

She checked every open window she passed. All were the same: empty, abandoned beds. Where were all the people who were supposed to be inside these houses? When had she seen characters acting strangely before...?

Not characters. *UNCs.* And there was only one reason a UNC would act out of character. They were going after Rico. She turned around and ran back for the village center.

She ran for nearly twenty minutes before she recognized the area where the party had been held. She ran past it towards the next section of the town.

A figure emerged in the darkness. Dorian.

"All the beds.... Empty..." Her lungs felt like they were filled with salt.

"What?"

She took a few seconds to let her breathing slow. "I checked a farming area on the other side of that hill, but I found something strange—all the beds are empty. It's like everyone just decided to wake up and get out of their beds in the middle of the night."

Dorian's face grew worried in the light of the torch. "UNCs."

"That means Rico's near the main plot," April said. "Or at least he was."

A whistle sounded off in the distance, but it was choked off. Randall.

"Come on," April said, and they sprinted towards the noise. The thought of Randall in trouble, of someone else being hurt under her watch, drove all thought of her burning lungs from her mind.

They seemed to run forever. Had they missed Randall? What if he had been in one of the houses they'd passed, in trouble and unable to call for help?

The sound of voices up ahead spurred her on. A throng of groundlings crowded outside one of the dwellings. Each groundling was dressed in old-fashioned pajamas. A few even wore stocking caps.

"Something tells me Randall's in there, or maybe Rico," April said. "But how do we get in?"

"Diplomacy," Dorian said. He cleared his throat loudly. "Ladies and gentlemen, your attention, please."

The throng of groundlings turned to face him. Their empty, unfocused eyes glinted creepily in the flickering torch light. She recognized the baker woman from earlier. Her eyes were just as glassy and lifeless as the others'. Was she asleep? Had the gate somehow hijacked her body? Or was she manipulated into thinking she was acting of her own free will?

"Are you crazy?" April whispered.

"Like you have any right to make judgement on my sanity," he whispered. He addressed the crowd. "I understand our friends have caused some problems for you. If you let us pass, we will take them and leave this place posthaste. We'll cause no further damage."

The throng continued to stare at them, no one spoke.

"I don't think it worked," April said.

"Give it a minute." He, too sounded nervous.

After a minute or so of glassy-eyed staring, the groundlings parted, leaving a path to the door open.

"Come on," Dorian said, relief in his voice. He grasped her hand and pulled her to the door.

"Be quick about it," a voice yelled from the throng. The rest of the crowd murmured in agreement.

Dorian pulled her more quickly, practically pushing her through the door before shutting it behind them. She hissed in pain as her head collided with the ceiling. She rubbed the spot, stooping over to avoid more damage.

"Randall?" she called. "Rico?"

"Hello?"

She held the torch up, casting dim light on Randall's face. He crouched low on his haunches. He looked like a grown man squatting in a child's playhouse. Rex sat on the ground next to him, his eyes flashing an iridescent green in the torchlight.

"Are you okay?" she asked.

Randall nodded. "I saw them crowding outside this house and thought Rico might be in here. I snuck in through a window in the back."

"Did you find him?" she asked, holding her breath.

Randall shook his head. "The place was empty. I think he was here but got scared when they showed up. He probably went out the same way I came in." he nodded towards the door. "Those things are freaky. Are they always like that?"

"UNCs," April said. "Unnamed characters. We'll explain later. Right now you just need to know that they are very, *very* protective of the storyline, or anything that might affect it."

"Oh," Randall said. "That makes sense."

"It does?"

He led them back to a small, groundling-sized desk. "Here." He lifted a journal. A sprawling signature on the cover read *Property of Braddy Evers.*

"Oh, no," Dorian said. "This keeps getting worse."

"Braddy Evers?" April asked, reaching for any residual pop culture she'd absorbed about the book. "You mean, like, the main character of this book? *The groundling?*"

"That's the one."

"So we're in the main character's house?"

Randall nodded. "It's also the setting for one of the most important scenes of the book—the scene where Labhras and the Nisser convince Braddy to accompany them on their quest."

"No wonder the UNCs are upset," April said.

"Hurry up in there," a voice called through the window. The crowd began to sound angry, restless.

"We have to hurry," Dorian said. "They won't tolerate our presence much longer."

"But Rico—"

Dorian shook his head. "We can't help him if we're dead. He's lost them. He'll be okay." He looked at Randall. "You're the strongest of the three of us," he said. "You have to grab one of them. If the gate closes for the day when there's such an imbalance, it will damage this world and ours."

"Once I grab one of them, we need to run," Randall said. "Something tells me they won't take kindly to kidnapping."

"But we can't just leave Rico!" she said.

"We don't have a choice," Dorian said.

"He's right," Randall's mouth was pressed in a thin line. "If they get us, then Rico's totally on his own. I'm sorry, April."

She glanced down at her watch. "We still have an hour left before the gate closes. We can go through the back window. Rico might be hiding in the woods, he might only be a few yards away..."

"It's too late for that," Dorian said.

April crossed her arms and planted her feet. "Well I'm not going."

Dorian and Randall exchanged a glance.

"Can you handle carrying one of those little guys?" Randall asked.

"I think so."

"Good." Randall scooped April up and tossed her over his shoulder.

"Let go of me!" she yelled, but he had her arms pinned against her sides. Most of the krav maga she knew hinged on the other person not expecting her to fight back, and Randall knew she was going to fight back.

"You'll thank me later," Randall said.

"I will not! Let me go!"

But Dorian was opening the door. "We're leaving," he yelled into the growing crowd. "The source of your malaise will soon be a distant memory..."

They walked through the crowd, Rex leading the way.

"Don't listen to them," April yelled at the crowd. "He's going to—"

But Randall clamped a hand over her mouth. "Do you have a death wish, girl?" he growled in her ear.

They walked cautiously to the edge of the mass of people. Dorian looked at them. "Get ready to run." He mouthed the words more than spoke them.

She and Randall cleared the edge of the mob. One figure stood a little further away from the rest. He seemed different than the others, less zombie-like. Quickly, Dorian grabbed him and hoisted him under his arm. He clamped a hand over the groundling's mouth, but not soon enough. The groundling eked out a startled, "Hey!"

It was all the motivation the mob needed to come after them with an angered roar.

"Go!" Dorian hissed, and they took off, the mob close on their heels.

Perhaps groundlings weren't the best runners—which made sense because of their short, stubby legs and squat frames—because they were able to keep some distance between them. It wasn't enough for them to be able to slow down, but as long as they didn't trip or fall or stop they'd get back to the gate with no problem.

This wasn't what April wanted at all.

They reached the square where the party had taken place earlier. They veered off into the woods towards the wine cellar.

Randall was barely able to slip through the portal holding her. Dorian followed, grunting under the groundling's weight.

"Put me down!" April screamed, kicking as hard as she could.

Randall said nothing, just continued to hold her. She was screaming so much that it took her a few seconds to realize that the groundling was doing the same.

"Barty!" Dorian said, "Do you mind?"

"Oh, right," Barty said, coming out of his shocked stupor. He raised his hands and spoke a few gibberish words. The groundling fell limp.

Barty looked at her nervously. "Uh, should I, uh, do her as well?"

"Don't you dare," she screamed.

"No need," Dorian said. "Look."

Randall turned her towards the portal and she stopped thrashing. The mob of groundlings had caught up with them. They stood on the other side of the portal, staring through it.

"If you go back through there they will tear you apart," Dorian said. "Then the boy will have no hope whatsoever."

"What would it matter?" April asked. "We're just leaving him there. They'll go after him, now."

Dorian shook his head. "Not necessarily. They all came after us. For all we know, they think he's with us now. If he keeps his head down we'll be able to find him tomorrow night."

Tomorrow night? How could she leave Rico there by himself for that long? He was alone and undoubtedly frightened. But what else could she do? She slumped in Randall's arms.

Randall, sensing her slackening limbs, said, "I'm going to let you go. Are you going to do anything stupid?"

She took a few moments before shaking her head.

Slowly, as though he didn't quite believe her, Randall loosened his grip. Her feet touched the floor, and he seemed poised to grab her if she made a run for the gate. She didn't. They were right. There was no way she could make it past that mob.

"Close it," Dorian said.

"No. Rico might try to come back. If he does..." It was already after four in the morning, there was less than an hour left before the portal would close, but there still might be time.

Dorian considered this for a moment before nodding. They watched the gate, and the groundlings watched them back.

At ten to five, Dorian spoke softly. "I have to go." Barty nodded and walked towards *The First Adventure of Braddy Evers,* closing it. April watched the gate shut on the staring faces of the groundlings, a tear rolling down her cheek. Dorian walked to the loose floorboard where *The Picture of Dorian Gray* was hidden. He pried the board loose and opened the book.

"What now?" Randall asked as the gate yawned open.

"We wait until evening," Dorian said. "The boy should be safe once the story moves on. Then we'll be able to find him and take him back here, no worse for wear."

April looked away. There were a lot of ways that plan could go wrong. What if the UNCs found him before then?

Barty pointed at the unconscious groundling. "What about him?"

"How long will he be asleep?" Dorian asked.

Barty lifted his chin. "Until I remove the enchantment."

Dorian nodded. "Good. Raoul will be here in a few minutes. Go downstairs, tell him you need the groundling someplace secure and safe for the rest of the say. He'll know what to do."

"Who's Raoul?" April felt so numb that it took her several seconds to realize that she'd been the one to say the words.

"The maintenance man," Dorian said.

Her breath caught in her throat. The last time Dorian had mentioned the word maintenance was the night they found Andre. He'd been the one to dispose of Andre's body and remove any evidence of his death from the library.

"Who is he, anyway?" April asked.

"Raoul is no ordinary custodian," he said. "Most people are unaware that the stipulations in Werner's will included one other employee who could not be fired."

"The janitor?" April asked. "Why?"

Dorian shrugged. "Not even Mae knew for sure, but what we've surmised over the years is he has a certain... skillset. He's the one we turn to when we're in a pickle." The clock began to chime. "I have to go, unless we want to mess things up more than we already have."

He stepped through the gate into the streets of nineteenth-century London. He remained facing them as the gate closed, his eyes meeting hers for the last few seconds before the crack met over them.

April stared at the stained-glass window for a few seconds, then tried to walk over to a chair to sit in it but stumbled. Her limbs felt heavy, like there were giant weights attached to them. Randall reached out and steadied her.

"Whoah—you need to get home and go to bed. You need some sleep before you come back for your shift."

"But the janitor—"

"Barty will take care of that."

Barty nodded. "Of course. Leave it to me."

Randall nodded to Barty. "I'm going to take her home."

"Wait," April said. "You'll need to lock up... where are the spare keys Rico brought in?..." she looked around desperately for them, but they were nowhere to be found. Rico must have brought them through the gate.

"Maintenance will lock up," Randall said. "Come on."

She wanted to protest more, but she was so tired... she allowed him to lead her down the stairs and out to her car. He deposited her in the passenger seat, like a father with a small child. It made her feel safe, like someone was taking care of all the big decisions.

He drove her home, leaving her car in the driveway. He watched her get into the house, and then walked down the street.

She trudged up to her room, sure there was no way she would sleep... but she fell diagonally onto her bed, her feet dangling over the edge, her head nowhere near the pillow. She was unconscious immediately.

Chapter Eight

Her eyes opened next a little more than an hour before she was supposed to be at work. She stumbled into the bathroom, wincing at the witch-woman staring back at her from the mirror. Her hair was matted and tangled, and her makeup had smeared down into raccoonish circles under her eyes. She made herself as presentable as possible, then walked out to the dining room.

Gram was eating lunch. She eyed April, and April knew she was going to say something. Luckily, she allowed her to make a sandwich and brew a pot of coffee first.

April sat down at the table with some trepidation. "Hey, Gram."

Gram murmured a greeting back but didn't immediately say what she had to say. Finally, when April was halfway through her sandwich, she said casually, "Do you have a boyfriend?"

"What?" The bite of turkey and bread that April had been working on almost fell out of her mouth. She forced herself to chew and swallowed. "Why would you think that, Gram?"

Gram shrugged. "You've been coming home so late these past couple of weeks. To tell you the truth, I've been a little happy about it. I think it's good, if you've found someone." She paused. "But it was quite a shock when I heard your car pull up at five thirty in the morning, look out, and see that Randall guy dropping you off in your car. Not only is he too old for you, I have to ask myself, what is April getting into that she can't even drive herself home?"

April's heart broke at Gram's worried expression. "Randall's just a friend, Gram. I wasn't feeling well so he dropped me off. He lives nearby."

"I see." Gram paused. "Well, you know I hate late risers," she fixed April with a stern look, "But I can't say the notion of you having a beau is a bad one."

"Really?"

"I'm not a nun, sweetie, and neither are you. You're a grown woman, and you've been working so hard... you deserve to have someone to take care of you."

April remembered the letter Gram had written. She'd mailed it the previous day. Would it hurt to let her think she had a boyfriend somewhere in the city? Until the ink rot was under control, April would be spending late nights at the library. It would be nice to have a cover story, something to tell Gram so that she wouldn't worry—and wouldn't scold her when she slept in until noon.

"Well, I didn't want to say anything, but I have met someone," April said. It was true, after all. Not that she could tell Gram that she'd been sleeping with a genie. "I wouldn't call him a boyfriend, though. Not yet."

To her surprise, Gram smiled. She looked relieved. "Oh, hon... that's great news."

"I didn't think you'd be so happy about it."

Gram grimaced. "I was pretty worried when you first started staying out so late. What can a girl your age be getting into that late at night? Nothing good. You have to admit this is the best-case scenario."

April winced, thinking of all she'd put Gram through. Gram needed to preserve her health; she shouldn't be worrying about April.

Gram continued. "But if it's not Randall, why did he drop you off?"

April shook her head, thinking fast. "Randall's his roommate, he, uh, works during the day and had to go to start his shift, so Randall had to drop me off—I was too tired to drive. That's also why we meet at night."

"Where did you meet him?"

"The library."

"What's he look like?" Gram said, leaning in and raising her eyebrows with a conspiratorial grin.

"You know—tall, dark, and handsome. Middle Eastern."

"What's his name?"

Oh, shit. "What?" April asked, completely caught off guard. She still didn't know the genie's name.

"You do know his name, right?" Gram was only half joking.

"Of course. It's... it's Dorian." April said the first name that popped into her head.

"Hmm. Dorian. Doesn't sound Middle Eastern."

"Yeah. One of his parents is American." It was amazing how easily the lies slipped from her mouth. She hated lying to Gram, but if this made Gram worry less...

"Well, I'd love to meet him sometime," Gram said.

"We'll try to arrange it," April said. "But like I said, he works during the day and you go to bed so early..."

Gram laughed and covered April's hand reassuringly with her own. "Don't worry, sweetie. Your old Gram won't embarrass you, and I understand if it's not a take-him-home-to-the-family situation. But if it does get serious... well, I'd just like to know the people who are important to you, is all."

"Okay, Gram."

Gram patted her hand. "Get a move on, now. You're going to be late for work."

April sighed. Work. Back to the library. She wished she could crawl back into bed and hide under the covers or disappear into *One Thousand and One Nights* for good. But she had to keep it together, for Rico's sake.

On her way to work, she found herself taking a longer route. She wasn't sure why until she passed Andre's apartment. She only knew which one it was because Andre would stop by the reference desk and say, *I stay just a block away at the Chateau Knoll Apartments. Nothing fancy, but it's clean and the neighbors are nice and quiet most of the time. I live on the top floor, corner apartment. Can see the library from my bedroom window.*

She slowed as she drove by. Only one apartment matched that description. Was his ex-wife inside, worried sick about her son? Had she realized he was missing yet?

When April walked into Mae's office, the first thing she noticed was a folded piece of paper set conspicuously on top of it. She picked it up. The note was written in small, precise print.

We have a problem. I'll meet you after close.
-Maintenance

Damn it. What could possibly be the matter? It had to be something to do with the groundling they'd abducted.

She didn't have much time to fathom what might have gone wrong because she saw Becky, accompanied by Rico's mom, enter the Werner Room. Rico's mom looked like she'd been up all night and hadn't showered that morning. They walked over to the reference desk and spoke with Janet. April groaned when they started walking towards her office.

Becky knocked. "Come in," April croaked, slipping the note into her desk drawer.

"Have you seen Rico? Andre's son?" Becky asked. Any anger she'd displayed towards April previously was absent, replaced with concern.

"He's been missing since last night," Rico's mom said, a desperate glint in her eyes.

April tried to screw her face up into a look of surprised concern. "Really? What time did you last see him?"

"Around nine. We got into a fight and he ran off." Her lips pressed into a regretful line. There was no trace of the overbearingness she'd exhibited the last time April had seen her. She just looked like a haggard mother whose child had gone missing. "I thought he was just blowing off steam. It's a safe neighborhood. I expected he'd be back within the hour. I didn't think..." her face crumpled, and Becky reached out an arm and patted her shoulder.

Rico's mom continued. "He went off in this direction. I thought maybe someone here saw him."

"I was at the library last night," April said, "I didn't see him."

"Did he say anything to you when he picked up Andre's stuff yesterday?" Becky asked.

April shook her head. "He just asked about his dad's things."

Rico's mom looked up. "Is it okay if I hang some fliers around the library? Maybe someone who comes in here has seen him..."

"Of course," Becky said. "You can use the staff printer. I'll show you where it is..."

When April went out to the desk, a flyer stand had been added to the array of brochures. A photocopied picture of Rico took up most of the page. *Have you seen this boy?* was written across the top. The picture was a school photo. In it Rico's hair was much shorter than it was now.

April sighed, angling the stand so she wouldn't have to see Rico's face. They'd get him back tonight. They'd somehow convince him not to say anything to anyone about being sucked into a book. Everything would go back to the crappy way it was before.

The rest of her shift passed agonizingly slowly. Randall nodded to her when he and Rex came in around six. She could feel him watching her out of the corner of his eye. Even Rex seemed to scrutinize her.

A couple other patrons who were in the room left, and then it was just her and Randall. He came up to the desk. "Did you get any sleep?"

She nodded. "I passed out as soon as I got to bed."

"You ready for tonight?"

"I think so."

He gave a forced laugh. "I guess that's all we can hope for, isn't it?"

He started to head back to his seat. She spoke. "Thanks. For dragging me out of there last night. I don't like it, but this is the best way to help Rico."

Randall nodded. "No problem."

Looking for a way to break the tension, she said, "Gram caught you dropping me off this morning. She was convinced you're my lover."

Randall's eyes raised. He cracked a grin. "I bet she was thrilled."

"She said you were too old for me."

"She's right about that. I could be your dad."

April told him about telling Gram that she had a boyfriend. He nodded at the information. "At least she won't worry."

"She's actually pretty excited by the idea. Unfortunately, she wants to meet my 'boyfriend' sometime."

Randall thought for a moment. "I suppose Barty could pose as your boyfriend..."

She laughed. "Right." She'd just have to figure out how to tell Barty that his name would be Dorian for the night.

~~~

After close, April showed Raoul's note to the others. Rex started to growl, and they turned to see what had riled him. A form emerged from shadows in the hallway.

The man had olive-toned skin and a pencil-thin moustache hugged his upper lip. His face was wrinkled and heavily lined, but he walked with the ease of a much younger man. Next to him was the groundling, who surveyed them with a scowl.

"Raoul," Dorian said, reaching out to shake the man's hand. "It's been a long time. I wish I could say it's good to see you."

"Raoul?" April asked. "You're the janitor?"

"Head of Maintenance," Raoul said, he offered his hand, and she took it. "It is a pleasure to meet you. You have large shoes to fill."

"Don't I know it," April said. "So you have the same sort of no-fire contract as Mae, right? Oswald Werner hired you."

Raoul nodded. "That's a story for another time. Right now, we have a bigger problem." He pointed to the groundling. "He woke up soon after Barty left this morning."

Dorian fixed Barty with a hard look. "Until you take it off, huh?"

Barty shrugged his shoulders sheepishly.

Raoul patted the groundling on the shoulder. "Go on. Tell them your name."

The small groundling stepped forward. "My name is Braddy Evers, and I do not take kindly to being pulled from my home in the middle of the night!"

"Braddy Evers," April said. "The main character? That shouldn't be possible, right?"

Dorian's face had lost all color. "It's not. He has to be there for the story to proceed."

"But... the grandfather paradox," April said. "If he's not there, what does that mean?"

"I don't know. This has never happened before."

"There are a couple possibilities," Barty said. "I'm no time travel expert, but it seems to me that if the story deviates from what's written in the book, then it's not the same world anymore."

"What does that mean?" Randall asked.

"It means that if we open *that* book"—he pointed to *The First Adventure of Braddy Evers*—"It won't go into the same world. This book can only take us to what's written inside of it."

"But Rico's in that world," April said. "What does that mean? Are you saying we can't get to the world where Rico is?"

"I'm sorry, April," Dorian said.

"We can't give up just because Barty has a theory," April said. "No offense, Barty." She looked at Dorian pleadingly. "Is there no hope at all?"

Dorian looked uneasy. "Time works differently in the books, as you know. The rate of difference fluctuates. It's possible that the next part of the story hasn't happened yet."

"It's possible that my theory is wrong," Barty said. "It's just a theory, after all."

The groundling—Braddy—crossed his arms. "And I would very much like to go back to my home and away from all this hullaballo, thank you very much!"

April nodded. She'd been thinking so much about getting Rico back she hadn't stopped to consider that they'd turned Braddy's life upside down, as well. "We'll get you back," she told him.

Randall rubbed his beard. "You must have been in bed when the boy broke into your house, right?"

Braddy nodded. "The sound woke me up. I thought it was drunkards from the party, so I called out and told them they had the wrong house. The noise only got louder, so I walked out to give them a piece of my mind. All my neighbors were standing at the doors and windows, but they weren't... themselves," he said, his brow furrowing. "As you can imagine, I wanted to get out of there. The boy was already climbing out the back window and that seemed as good an exit as any. He ran off, and I circled around to the front to see what the blazes was going on." He glared up at Dorian. "That's when I was snatched off the very ground I was standing on."

"Did you see where the boy ran?" April asked.

"Off into the woods. I didn't watch him much further than that. He'd broken into my home, after all." Braddy fell into a chair, crossing his arms disapprovingly. The chair dwarfed him so that he looked like a pouting child.

"We have to go back in," April said. "We have to see if Rico is still there."

Randall, Barty, and Dorian all looked between each other. Dorian spoke. "Perhaps Randall and I should go alone. You and Braddy stay here with Barty."

"*What?*" April and Braddy said in unison.

"I'm not staying here!" the groundling exclaimed. "I'm going home."

"I'm not staying here, either," April said. "This is my fault. I'm going to be the one to fix this."

Dorian crossed his arms. He ignored Braddy and focused on April. "You are too close to this problem," he said. "You are emotionally invested in it in a very dangerous way."

"Please." She gripped his hands and stared into his eyes imploringly, and as she did, something in his gaze softened.

"What if Rico isn't there, April? Will you be able to handle it?"

She nodded. "I was weak yesterday. I'll keep it together." Dorian didn't look convinced, so she added, "I'm the Pagewalker. If I can't do this, what am I?"

Dorian closed his eyes. "Fine. But you must listen to me, otherwise we're taking you right back." He glanced at Randall. "Right?"

Randall nodded. "Sacrificing yourself won't help get him back, okay?" The hard look in his eyes reminded her of his story about losing his partner in Afghanistan. She got the feeling that in some way, he was trying to protect her from what had happened to him.

She nodded. "Okay."

"What about me?" Braddy said, stretching up to be in their field of vision. "I want to go home!"

With a sigh, Dorian crouched down in front of the groundling. "Let me explain to you what this additional universe means to you. It means there's quite possibly *another* Braddy in your bed, drinking your tea and eating your scones. There can't be two of you."

Braddy sputtered. "That Braddy needs to find his own house!"

"You'll stay here with Barty," Dorian said, a tone of finality in his voice. "We'll assess things. If it's safe, we'll bring you back and you can to spend the rest of your days eating and sleeping to your heart's content."

"Well, not really," Randall said. "I mean, in the *book...*"

Dorian shook his head. "He can deal with that later." He glanced around at everyone. "We're all in agreement, then?"

Except for Braddy, everyone nodded. Raoul spoke. "I must go. I have other matters to attend to. Let me know in the morning if you need my assistance."

Dorian nodded. "I hope I won't have cause to see you for many more years."

"Me too," Raoul said, but he glanced at April in a doubtful way that she tried not to take offense to.

After Raoul left, they readied to head back into *The First Adventure of Braddy Evers*. Braddy began to protest again, but Barty threatened to knock him out with another sleep spell.

"Because that worked so swimmingly last time," Dorian muttered. Still, it was enough to make Braddy sit back down in the chair, his arms crossed and his legs sticking out like matchsticks.

After stepping through the gate, April began searching for signs that the world had reset itself. She moved to the edge of the wood. The dining area was empty and abandoned.

"There's no party," she said. "If the world reset, then the party would be happening again, right?"

"Not necessarily. The party wasn't described in the book. It's not necessary that everything about the world be the exact same, only that those things described in the book's text are."

"But it's still possible for this to be the same world, right?"

"Yes. It's definitely a good thing that the party isn't happening."

April nodded. He was right, but she didn't let herself give up hope. It wasn't proof that that the world was the same, but it wasn't proof of the opposite, either.

"Come on. We need to get to Braddy's house."

They set off. The town looked different in full daylight. The mammoth trees over groundlings' dwellings were covered in yellow-green moss, and many had multi-colored flowers growing all around them. If she had time to stop and appreciate the scenery she would have thought it was the perfect place for a picnic.

They passed groundlings gardening, or, more often, napping in the sunshine that filtered through the treetops. The ones who were awake waved to them.

"Weird," April said. "They wanted to kill us yesterday."

They walked in silence. Randall pointed to one of the tree dwellings. "That's it."

"Are you sure?" she asked. Everything looked so different in the daylight that it was hard to tell.

He pointed to a small wooden sign in the yard. The words *Ever Home* were carved into it. "In the book that was the name of Braddy's house."

"Oh." She looked down at the ground. The path outside of Ever Home was marred with footprints, more than the rest of the path. They must have been left by the previous night's mob. Or maybe that was just her being hopeful....

"Braddy said Rico ran into the woods out back," Dorian said. "Let's check there. If he's smart, he'll have stayed hidden."

They walked around the house calling Rico's name.

"It's April," she called. "If you can hear us, please come out."

They searched the woods behind the house for hours. When her voice became hoarse, she checked her watch. It was nearly midnight in the library. Why did it seem like time was moving so fast?

"I'm going to check the house," Randall said finally. He walked back through the woods towards the dwelling.

April sat down on a log. "We're not going to find him," she said.

Dorian came and sat next to her. "We still have time." He didn't sound convinced of his own words.

"You don't think we'll find him," she said.

Dorian took a few seconds to answer. "Maybe not today. But I promise you, we won't give up. Even if this isn't the same world, we'll find a way. Okay?"

She nodded.

"Guys!" Randall yelled. "Come here—quick!"

Dorian and April jump to their feet. They ran through the woods and into the house. April stopped as soon as she opened the door. The house was a complete mess.

"Oh, no," she said, taking a step backwards. "The UNCs...?"

Randall shook his head and smiled. "No, it's not like that. This is a *good* thing."

"It is?"

"You see, one of the first scenes in *The First Adventure of Braddy Evers* is Labhras the magician inviting a bunch of Nisser to Braddy's house. They cook and basically make a huge mess."

April wasn't sure what a Nisser was, but she didn't want to take the time to ask. She examined the scene more closely. Dishes stacked in the sink, overturned wine barrels, smatterings of food remnants on the floor... Randall was right. It looked more like the aftermath of a party than a mob of zombified townsfolk tearing a house apart. Still, the vice grip on her heart didn't loosen.

"But that's not possible," she said. "Braddy's been with Raoul. There has to be another explanation."

Dorian nodded. "You're right. Something else must have happened."

Randall grabbed something on the desk. Next to an open quill well was a piece of parchment. Written on the parchment in splotchy, inelegant print were the words:

April,

I'm going on an adventure.

-R

"R?" April said. "Rico? But how's that possible?"

Dorian looked down at the note, his brow furrowed. "There's 'not possible,' and then there's 'already happened.'"

"Wait," Randall said. "What's happened?"

Dorian chewed on the inside of his lip. "By all appearances, this story has moved on, but how's that possible when the main character is sequestered in the library? Judging by this note, Rico has somehow *overtaken* Braddy's role."

"What does that mean?" She asked.

"I'm not sure. We need more information."

She looked down at the note. At least they were in the right world, but was this really any better? It was dangerous. She didn't know much about *The First Adventure of Braddy Evers*, but she knew there were evil creatures around, including dragons, pixies, and other terrifying creatures. How could Rico survive all that? And on top of that, if he slipped up, the UNCs would be after him.

"But you said that everything has to happen exactly as described in the book!" April said. "How's that possible when it's Rico and not Braddy?"

Dorian slammed his fist down on the table. "I don't know! Maybe he's Braddy's twin. Maybe they're two groundlings with the same name." He paused. "I think the gate is doing what it can to protect itself."

Everyone was quiet, thinking that over.

April broke the silence. "Can we find him?"

Dorian ran his fingers through his blond curls. "It's possible. Though with how inconsistently time passes in the story worlds it will be difficult to locate him."

"Guys," Randall said from behind them. He held up Rico's note. He pressed the pad of one finger to the ink. It came away smudged with black. "The ink's still wet. He just wrote this."

"Then they can't have gone far," Dorian said. "We could still catch up with them."

"Let's not waste any time," April said. "Randall—are you familiar enough with the story to know where they went?"

Before he could answer, a small shriek ensued from outside. "Stop!" The voice yelled. "It's me, Braddy Evers! This is my house!"

They jumped up and bounded outside. Braddy stood in the road, a mob of townsfolk standing in a circle around him.

"You shouldn't be here," one of the zombified voices said.

"Yeah. You're an abomination."

"I *live* here!" Braddy said, simultaneously indignant and terrified. "The Evers are the most respectable family in all of Groundsville! You always know what to expect from an Evers!"

The mob closed in on him.

Braddy appealed to one of the groundling women standing closest to him. "Willie, you come over for tea at least once a week!" When Willie didn't acknowledge him, Braddy looked at them desperately. "Help!"

April looked down the road, the one Rico had just ridden down, according to Randall. For all they knew he might only be a ten-minute walk away. Some of the townsfolk who had crowded around Braddy were now shambling in that direction, forming a line across the road. There was still enough space for them to get through...

"Help!" Braddy cried.

She couldn't just leave him. With a frustrated growl, April turned to help Braddy. Small hands grabbed her arms, but she easily knocked them away with a jerk of her wrists. She used enough force that the groundlings tumbled to the ground.

"Sorry," she said to them, wincing. It was like pushing down kids. They rose without a word, their vacant eyes fixed in her direction.

Randall also approached Braddy. One by one, he grabbed the groundlings by the shirt collar and tossed them gently to the side of the road, which was cushioned by tall, lush grass. When he got to Braddy, he picked him up.

"It's probably safest if I carry you," Randall said. "You guys don't seem to run that fast."

"Fine," Braddy said, terrified. "Just get me out of here. What's wrong with them? These are my neighbors, my friends!"

"There's more of them." Dorian nodded to the road up ahead. More groundlings were coming from the opposite direction. Unlike the groundlings surrounding them now, these ones carried weapons and tools. One held a pitchfork, others kitchen knives of various sizes. One woman in a dirt-smeared apron gripped an oversized pair of garden shears in both hands.

"Something tells me they're going to be harder to overpower," Randall said. He pushed away the groundlings who had come back and were beating his hips with their tiny fists. The blows didn't seem to do much damage to him, but Braddy scrambled up onto his shoulders with a yelp.

"We have to get back to the gate," Dorian said. As though he knew what she was thinking, he said to April, "We'll open the book to the next scene. It's Rico's best chance."

He was using Rico to manipulate her, but he was right. She nodded. They started running, but after a few hundred yards, she realized they weren't being followed. She slowed.

"Why aren't they coming after us?" she asked.

Dorian and Randall slowed and turned around to see the line of groundlings off in the distance.

"We can't affect the plot from here," Dorian said. "They only need to keep us from taking that stretch of road."

"Maybe we can sneak around them by going through the woods," she said.

The second the words came out of her mouth, the door to the nearest dwelling opened and two groundlings came out, a man and a woman. The man held an axe that looked like it was meant for chopping firewood. They stopped, obviously waiting for them to try to leave the path.

"They won't let us," Dorian said. "Our best bet is to skip to the next scene." He said the last part in a whisper so that the UNCs couldn't hear him.

April watched the man with the axe nervously as they hurried back to the gate. More groundlings came and lined the road as they walked past, guarding the edge of the path. They followed them into the woods and to the gate. Even after they stepped through the veil, the UNCs remained on the other side, watching, guarding.

Braddy stared at the faces of the nearest groundlings. He pointed to one of them. "Paid for his son's schooling, I did. A fine way to repay me!"

"Don't hold it against him," April said. "He's not really the same guy right now. The gate has sort of... taken over his body." She turned around. "Where's Barty?"

At that moment Barty walked up through the door. He held a paperback book in his hands. He looked surprised to see them. "Oh, you're back already? Did you find the boy?" He started to look nervous as he noticed their angry glares.

"Where have you been?" Randall asked.

Barty rubbed his neck nervously. "Braddy didn't believe that this book was really written about him. He said no respectable Evers would ever go questing. He wanted to read the book, but I told him it had to stay open so you guys could come back. I went downstairs and got a paperback copy." He held up the book. "Why? Did something happen?"

"Yeah," Dorian said. "Your charge snuck through the portal, alerting the UNCs to our presence. We missed a chance to reach Rico." He raised his index finger in the air and waved it back and forth emphatically. "The next person who leaves someone unattended in this room..." he seemed to be searching for a suitable threat, but couldn't, so he ended with an angry puff of air.

Randall rubbed his chin. "Would it have mattered? We'd need Braddy along to replace Rico anyway. If we had tried to just take him, the UNCs would still have come after us."

Dorian nodded. "You're right," he sighed. "They might not be happy if we remove him—even to make the switch with the real Mr. Evers."

"We have to try, though, right?" April said.

Dorian nodded. "We will try. I don't know what it means that Rico was able to slip into a named role—*the* named role."

"I'm less worried about that right now than I am about getting him back."

"You're right. Let's leave the philosophy for later." Dorian turned to Randall. "You read a lot. Do you know what happens next?"

Randall thought. "It's been a while since I last read this book... I believe the first obstacle Braddy faces in the book is a baobhan sith that enters the adventure party's camp."

"Baobhan sith?" April asked.

"An Irish vampire."

"Ah," April said. "Why do they want Braddy to join their quest, anyway?"

"They need a sneak-thief."

She raised her eyebrow.

"Someone who loots treasure."

Braddy spluttered. "I would do no such a thing! I wouldn't sneak-thief in general, especially not a baobhan sith."

"According to the book, you do," Barty said. He was thumbing through the paperback.

"Nonsense! Give me that." He snatched the paperback out of Barty's hands and settled down into one of the armchairs. "And some tea and biscuits would be nice, if you're set on holding me captive." He began to read with a sour look on his face.

"There's no time," April said. "We need to go." She grabbed the hardcover version of *The First Adventure of Braddy Evers* and flipped it open to the second chapter. The crack in the stained-glass window appeared with a pop. She flipped through the pages as it widened. With the turn of each page, the gate emitted a *whomping* sound and a series of vibrations ran beneath their feet.

"Can you not do that?" Barty asked. He glanced at the gate, the expression on his face suggesting he expected it to explode.

April ignored him. "I think it's best to try to get to him *before* they encounter the vampire, don't you agree? Then we can make the switch."

Braddy's face had gone white in the armchair. He was reading the book, his small eyes shocked. "They are riding through freezing wind and rain! They made me wear Nisser clothes... and... there's water dripping in my eyes... and they're drinking all my tea!" He crossed his arms. "I'm half a mind to stay here where it's warm and safe."

Dorian shot the groundling a look. "Five minutes ago all you could talk about was going back to your world. Here's your chance. Don't you want adventure?"

Braddy lifted his chin. "An Evers never seeks excitement," he said. "An Evers prides himself in being predictable and never doing anything surprising."

"Right," Dorian said. "Maybe it's best if we leave him here while we look around. Once we figure out where they are, we'll sneak him through and make the switch before the UNCs realize what's happening." He paused. "The groundlings were relatively harmless, but the last thing we want to deal with are UNC pixies or wurms intent on killing us."

April shivered at the thought, but Randall rubbed his chin. "I don't know," he said. "I wouldn't mind seeing a wurm."

Dorian rolled his eyes. "You think that until you see one."

April shook her head. "We're wasting time." She turned to Dorian. "No matter what, we're going to go through the portal at the time shown in the book, right?"

Dorian shook his head. "Not necessarily. Now that we've witnessed part of the action, it's probable that we're locked into time with it, meaning that time there is moving relative to ours."

"Has any other book ever been locked like this?" April asked.

"Only one that I know of. Mine."

"Oh." April decided to consider the revelation about Dorian's world later. "So there's a possibility of missing them?"

"It's impossible to know for sure."

"I think this is as good a spot as any." The text on the page described Braddy (*Rico*, she thought in her head) and the Nisser riding their ponies through rainy weather in the forest. She wasn't looking forward to the rain and cold, but at least there weren't any trolls.

She placed the book on the table. Once they stood in front of the gate, she turned back to Barty. "We'll be back soon. Don't let him out of your sight."

Braddy glanced up from his book. "If you lot want to be out fighting baobhan sith and whatnot in the bitter cold, be my guests. I'll be here where it's warm."

They walked through the gate again. April allowed herself a few seconds to marvel that she barely noticed the transition. A little more than three weeks ago she hadn't known the gate existed. Now she was walking through the veil as blithely as if she were stepping into an elevator.

Icy drips of rain pelted her skin. She thought of her warm coat hanging uselessly on the peg in her office. She shivered.

Focus. You need to keep an eye out for Rico.

They walked around, and she looked behind her. The gate had appeared in a small cave set between two large boulders that leaned against each other. They were surrounded by trees.

"Where's the road?" Randall asked. They looked around. They didn't appear to be near the road at all.

"It must be close," April said. "We probably can't see it through the trees. Come on..."

"Curious."

They looked up to the tops of the boulders at the source of the voice. A tall man in a fitted black jacket complete with tails crouched on top of the boulder. He peered down at them intently. The oversized top hat on his head did little to stop the rain from dripping into his eyes, though the inclement weather didn't seem to bother him. In his right hand he grasped a wand.

Rex whined nervously, as though the magician had taken even him by surprise.

"It's Labhras," April said.

"How do you know, Miss I-don't-read?" Randall asked.

"Rico pointed him out last night."

"True," the tall magician said. "I am Labhras, and Labhras is me. I am pleased that you know my name. But the true question is, what are three groundlings doing out in the wilderness—in a storm, no less—so far from Groundsville? Any magician worth his wand knows groundlings prefer to stay indoors with a warm fire, a generous plate of scones and a steaming pot of tea." He leaned in closer to them. "Or maybe you're not groundlings at all. Perhaps you merely look like them."

They stared at each other, each wondering how to answer Labhras' question. The lack of response angered the magician. He snapped his fingers, and the sound of thunder erupted from them. For a moment the clatter drowned out the storm. Any person for miles around would have heard the crack and remarked at it being a particularly loud crack of thunder.

Rex barked, a high-pitched sound, and then crouched behind Randall's legs.

The others looked at April. She was the Pagewalker, after all. She stepped forward. "The... *power* that sent us protects us by masking our true appearance. We mean no harm."

"The power?" Labhras mused. "You mean the door beneath my feet? The one that leads somewhere and nowhere at all?"

April wasn't sure what he meant, and at the same time it made a strange sort of sense. She nodded, though she wasn't sure he saw the gesture because he continued to speak.

"And what is a door for, if not to be opened and walked through? Who are you in relation to this door?" he gestured to her with his staff, and she fought the urge to shrink back, remembering the thunder-like clatter it had made a few seconds earlier.

Who was she? "I... I am the one who walks through it. I am the one who opens it." She gestured to Dorian and Randall. "And these are my friends. They help me with the... walking through and opening."

Labhras nodded. "So it is. And why did you walk through this particular door?"

April rushed to answer. Perhaps Labhras could help them get Rico back. "Our friend was taken by a party of Nisser. It is a mistake that he is here. We need to find him."

"You mean Mr. Evers?" Labhras mused.

She nodded. "Can you help us?"

He ignored her question. "It was no mistake that he started this journey. I am the one who sent him on it."

"What?" April looked at Randall. He'd told her that in the book Braddy had gone on a journey with a group of Nisser in search of treasure. "Why?"

"Why, indeed." He punctuated the question with a short *ha*. "I could sense something in him. For all his finery and teas, he was not like the other groundlings. I could sense that he *needed* an adventure, mayhaps more than the Nisser needed a serviceable sneak-thief. I'd been searching these parts for days and hadn't found a single groundling who would do, even in a pinch. Then I found Braddy."

"But he's not really Braddy!" April shouted.

For a moment there was a look like thunder in the magician's eyes, and April shrank back from him. But then he seemed to consider her words.

"Not really Braddy... hmm..." he worried the rounded top of his staff. "Well you're right about that, and you're also not."

"What? How can I be both right and not right at the same time?"

"When your friend is at once Braddy and not Braddy, just as you are groundlings and not groundlings."

"But he's *not*," April insisted.

"He is for the time being, at least," Labhras said.

"So what should we do?" Dorian yelled from behind her.

"You must wait until the adventure is complete. Then you can get your friend back."

"But we need him back *now*!" April said.

"You will have to wait. You don't have much choice in the matter." He pressed his lower lip upwards as though thinking about something. "Who knows? Maybe one adventure can become two."

"*What?*"

Labhras ignored her question. "The road is a few paces in that direction. If you walk down it, the adventure party, of which your not-Braddy is currently a member, is about ten minutes away. They had just passed by when you came out of your door from nowhere."

"Thank you," April said, relieved to finally get a helpful, non-gibberish answer out of him. "Come on, guys. Let's go."

Labhras shook his head with a chuckle. "But I wouldn't recommend it. There are dangerous creatures in these woods."

"Well, that's just fine," April said. She was about to tell Labhras that she was tired of all the riddles and roundabout answers, but a flash of lighting struck somewhere behind the magician. When the light faded from their eyes, Labhras was gone.

"That was annoying," she said. "Let's go." She stepped towards the road in the direction Labhras had indicated, but Randall and Dorian didn't immediately follow her. "What are you waiting for?"

"Labhras said not to go that way," Dorian said.

Randall nodded. "You haven't read *The First Adventure of Braddy Evers,* but I have. Labhras is a smart dude. He might be vague and archaic sometimes, but he generally gives good advice, and he's always on the side of the greater good."

Dorian shook his head. "It may appear that way, but I've read articles in journals where Labhras is painted in a not-so-great light—"

April started to walk towards the road. "Guys, I'm going. With or without you."

The scuffling behind her told her that Randall and Dorian were following her. After a few paces, she emerged onto a wide dirt path. Hoof prints in the mud were barely visible as the rain quickly melted them away.

April clapped her hands. Rico was just up the road from them. All they had to do was follow, and soon he'd be home, safe. She was about to turn to the others and ask if they thought it was best to go and grab Braddy from the library when the trees on the left side of the road about fifty paces ahead began to rustle. Some of the trees were at least thirty feet high.

April watched in horror as two large creatures moved out. They were three times taller than Randall. They were humanoid in only the most basic ways: each had a head, two arms, and two legs. But their heads were lumpy and bulbous, their arms long, gangling, and wiry. They stared with dull, vacant eyes.

"UNCs," Dorian said.

"Trolls," Randall said.

"UNC trolls," April finished.

"We have to go back," Dorian said. "We'll try again at a later point in the story."

"That's what we've been doing," April said. "It's not working. We're just going to keep doing this and being one step behind until—"

"Until we find him," Dorian said, "But we'll find him. I promise we will."

Up ahead, the trolls began to lumber towards them. It looked like they weren't going to wait for April, Randall, and Dorian to make a move.

Without any other choice, they turned back, running for the two gray boulders the gate had wedged itself between. Through the veil they could see Barty and Braddy sitting at the table nearest the gate. Barty tapped at his phone nervously; Braddy frowned down at *The First Adventure of Braddy Evers* paperback.

They heard the thundering steps of the trolls behind them.

"Go!" Randall said, and he pushed her through the veil, Rex coming right after her. He and Dorian followed. No sooner had they turned around and looked back through the gate then they saw clubs smashing against the small opening. Drops of water from the ends of their clubs splashed onto the hardwood floor.

April spluttered, trembling from a mixture of cold and frustration. She looked at Randall and Dorian. They, too, were pale and washed-out. At least Randall had his coat on—a perk of always having your possessions on you. Rex shook, splashing them all with muddy water.

"Let's go to the next scene," April said. She walked towards the book, but Dorian stopped her.

"We need to dissect what just happened," he said. "Acting rashly will not help us."

April wanted to resist, to tell them that they needed to get back inside the book *now*, but her own freezing limbs stopped her. Her body insisted in remaining in the warm library, which felt like a sauna after standing in the freezing rain and wind.

"Yeah," Randall said. "How did Labhras know about the gate, anyway?"

April had wondered the same thing, but she'd already formed a theory on the matter. "I think that magical beings can sense the gate." She explained about the genie and how he'd been able to see through her disguise the first time she met him.

"But Labhras wasn't able to see through our disguises—he only sensed that we weren't what we said we were."

"It must work differently based on each book."

Randall nodded. "Makes sense, in a way. The magic of the realms is subtler than, say, that of *Harry Potter*. I haven't read *One Thousand and One Nights,* but I'm guessing the same principle may apply there." Randall turned to Barty.

"You're a warlock," he said. "Can you tell that something is different about Braddy?" he gestured to the small groundling, who was still reading the book, the frown lines on his face growing deeper.

"Aside from the fact that he's half my height? No."

Dorian shook his head. "When a character crosses over into the library they don't arrive in disguise. It only works the other way around. That's not—"

"Guys," April said. "For every second that passes here, minutes, maybe *hours,* pass over there. We need to go back in, *now.*"

"She's right," Dorian said. "But we need warmer clothes."

"I have my winter coat," April said. "Randall's already wearing his. Let's see..." she walked over to the reference desk and pulled out the lost and found. Inside was a windbreaker, and several mismatched gloves. She pulled a couple of the gloves out along with the windbreaker and brought them over to Dorian, who gazed down at them with distaste.

"I suppose it's better than freezing to death," he said, taking them out of her hands. He grimaced as he zipped the windbreaker. "Smells like tobacco smoke. Let's go."

They flipped ahead a few pages, the gate *whomping* with each turn. They chose a page where the adventure party had stopped to camp for the night.

"Something's wrong," Randall said, looking through the gate. April could hear the frown in his voice. "It's daylight. It should be night."

April glanced at the text in the book. He was right.

"Well, let's see what's going on," April said. The others nodded. They walked through the gate.

The rain had stopped, though the *drip, drip* of the remaining water escaping the canopy above their heads surrounded them. Early-morning sunlight filtered yellow-green through the treetops.

The gate had opened in the mouth of a makeshift shelter beneath a large stone overhang jutting out from a hill. The ground was littered with the signs of an abandoned camp: broken twigs, shelters, and other various refuse. Near the edge of the overhang was a firepit filled with ash and blackened wood.

"They've left," Dorian said. "The story has moved on from here."

Damn it. April kicked the pile of dripping sticks. When were they going to get Rico back?

"What's that?" Randall was looking at the back of the cave. April squinted in that direction. She saw something that looked like a boulder, but there was something strange about it...

"It's a woman," she said, seeing the curve of the knees and the angle of elbows held over the woman's face as though to protect her eyes from unbearably bright light. "She may need help."

The woman remained perfectly still as April approached. She hadn't moved since they'd entered the cave. And why was she pallid, almost gray?

"She's... a statue?" April said, stopping a couple feet from the woman. She reached out to touch her, but then pulled her hand away, thinking better of it.

"The baobhan sith," Randall said.

"The vampire?" April said, stepping away from the woman.

"Yes. In the book she turns to stone when the sun touches her."

"Sun turns vampires into stone?" April asked.

"At least baobhan sith."

April stared down at the woman. "We should go back to the library," she said.

They were about to head back to the gate when something in the clearing caught April's eye. It was a triangular pile of rocks set at the head of a rectangle of overturned earth. A grave.

"No!" she ran towards it, stopping next to it. There was no mistaking it for what it was. It was so fresh that the mound of dirt hadn't yet collapsed downwards.

Dorian, Randall, and Rex ran up beside her.

"It's not Rico," Randall said.

Dorian nodded. "He's the title character. The title character can't die."

"Then who is it?" April asked, her voice croaking.

Randall screwed up his face. "I think one of the Nisser fell victim to the baobhan sith, but I'm not sure."

"You're not *sure*?" April asked. "How can someone die in a children's book?"

Everyone was silent. They stared down at the grave. Randall said, "What do we do now?"

"We go back to the library and head them off at the next scene," April said.

Dorian shook his head. "No. That's what we've been doing, and it hasn't worked."

"What, then?" April asked, tired of trying to come up with solutions to a problem that she was rapidly beginning to believe was unsolvable. *You can't think like that,* she reminded herself. *Keep trying for Rico.*

"We're always one step behind," Dorian said. "Too much about this world is taking us by surprise."

"And how do you propose we solve that?" April asked, crossing her arms.

"How many copies of *The First Adventure of Braddy Evers* does the library own?" Dorian asked. "At least three?"

Randall nodded. "A popular book like that, yeah."

"Wait," April said. "Rico is trapped in this world and you want to sit in the library and *read*?"

"We need to learn more about this world. We need to read, note down details, and then make a plan. No more flailing about."

"But that means Rico has to face *whatever* happens in the next chapter by himself."

"Fairies." Randall said.

"What?"

"The next chapter takes place in the fairy city."

"If you know that, what's the point of us all going back and reading?"

"We should all know what's going on," Dorian said. "Not just Randall. One of us might see something that he doesn't, and he can't always be around to explain things to us."

April turned to Randall. "What do *you* think about this?"

Randall looked between them, then finally breathed out. "He's right. We can't keep doing the same thing and expect different results. To be honest, it's been a while since I read this book, and I could use a refresher."

Any hope that April had of Randall backing her up dissipated. She looked off into the distance, wondering which direction Rico had gone. How far away was he? He could be just over the next hill, or through the trees...

But that wasn't a sure thing, was it? He could also be miles away. Their best bet was to meet them at a future page with a plan.

"You're right," she said. She glanced down at the timepiece. "It's already two. We should get started. We have a long night ahead of us."

When they made it back into the library, Barty and Braddy were missing. They soon returned, though, Braddy carrying a small pot of tea and Barty a package of cookies from the staff cupboard.

"The biscuits aren't fresh," the groundling said with a sniff, "But these are desperate times."

Randall collected all the copies of *The First Adventure of Braddy Evers* from the second and first floors. With all the editions that had been published over the years, there were enough for each of them to have their own copy three times over. They retired to the sitting area. Dorian went back into his world and returned with blankets, and they wrapped themselves in them, hoping to regain the feeling in their cold-numbed limbs.

"Wait," she said as he handed her a quilt. "You didn't bring anything over there. How can these be here?"

"As long as the gate is active it's fine," he said. "It's when the gate closes for the day that the trouble starts."

He looked away, and she remembered the fight they'd had the previous night.

"Oh," she said.

For the next hour, the only sounds in the Werner Room were the flipping of pages, the slurp of tea, or the occasional clearing of a throat.

Every so often Braddy would mutter, "Utterly preposterous." The groundling clutched his blanket at his neck as though he were reading a horror story rather than a children's book.

Soon April's head began to throb. She took a break to check her watch. It was nearing three in the morning. She'd read faster than she'd ever read anything in her life, and she'd only managed to get halfway through the book. She set it aside and massaged her temples with the tips of her fingers, trying to ease the pounding.

She flipped back to the beginning of her book. "What happens if you open a Werner book to an author's note?"

Dorian grimaced. "It's very... abstract. Difficult to describe. You'll see for yourself soon enough."

Randall closed his own book with a sigh. Out of all of them, he'd read the furthest. "Why don't we get some rest?" he said. "We can finish during the day tomorrow. Anyway, we won't remember what we read if we don't sleep."

"You don't have to twist my arm," she said. She blinked. Her eyelids felt dry and sticky, and she had to fight to pry them open again. "Do you need a ride?"

Randall shook his head. "No. I'll walk to the shelter. It's only a few blocks away."

April gazed levelly at him. She knew that St. Mary's locked its doors by ten p.m. and didn't open again until nine the next morning. Where was he going to spend the night? For that matter, where had he been sleeping the past few weeks? It wasn't as cold out as it had been—thank goodness—but it was still Minnesota in November.

As though reading her thoughts, Randall said, "I'll be fine. I know some spots."

She nodded. "If you ever need a place, you know where I live, okay?"

He nodded, though she knew he wouldn't take her up on it. Then he leaned down and ruffled the fur around Rex's neck. "What do you say, boy? Are you ready to go?"

The dog yawned and let his head fall back onto the floor with a sigh. Everyone laughed, but only a little. April could tell that the next night's activities were looming in their minds as much as they were in hers.

"What about me?" Braddy asked. "Don't I deserve a warm bed?"

Dorian sighed. "You'll stay with me until the morning, then Raoul will come back and watch you for the rest of the day."

The groundling's look of distaste showed that he didn't much like the idea of spending the day with Raoul. Barty added, "If you want, I could knock you out again." This was said as a genuine offer, not a threat.

The groundling looked at him as though he were insane. "No, thank you. I'll sleep here." He patted the couch he was sitting on.

Barty and Randall left, leaving April, Dorian, and Braddy. Braddy was already spread out on the couch, his blanket pulled up over his head.

"There's still time," Dorian said absently.

"Time for what?"

"To go visit him. There's an hour left before the portal closes. That's at least a couple hours there."

"Where? And who do you mean by *him?*" she asked, then realization crept over her, and heat flooded her cheeks. "You mean the genie? Why would I go there now?"

"I thought it might be... I don't know, stress release."

"Rico is trapped in a book, and we're unable to get to him," April said shortly. "The last thing on my mind is a..." she looked for the right word and got a flash of the conversation she'd had with the genie the first time she'd seen him. "The last thing on my mind is a booty call."

Dorian's face was even more florid than hers felt. "Oh."

"Why do you care, anyway?"

He looked into the gate. "I just wanted you to know I support your decisions. Whatever you need." He didn't look at her again.

She tried to think of something else to say about that conversation, but couldn't, so she just continued to look at the gate with him. "You'll leave it open as long as possible?" She asked finally. "Just in case?"

He nodded. "Yes." He didn't look at her again.

Chapter Nine

"You're awfully tired this morning. Did you have a good time last night?" Gram asked with a suggestive smile.

April tried not to wince at the comment coming from her grandmother. She simply agreed with Gram's statement, though it was the furthest thing from the truth, and returned to *The First Adventure of Braddy Evers,* which lay open on the kitchen table in front of her.

"I haven't seen you read since high school," Gram commented. "In fact, I don't recall you reading *in* high school. This library thing must be growing on you, huh?"

"Yes, Gram," April said. "Braddy Evers Day is coming up and I thought I should read it before then."

"Well, good." Gram said with a smile. "I'm glad to see you developing more interests and hobbies lately." She returned to her newspaper. "Did you hear about this kid who went missing near the library?"

April dropped the book so fast that she lost her page. "What?"

"His name is Rico," Gram kept reading, then she looked up at April and started to read out loud. "'His father, a security guard at the local library, went missing last week. Authorities suspect that the boy may be in his father's custody.'"

"Man," April said, her mouth dry. "His mom came in yesterday looking for him. We all thought he ran away, that he'd be back before it got dark out. I can't believe he's still missing."

Gram shook her head. "First that man walks out on his job, then kidnaps his son right out from under his mother's nose? Some people."

April winced. Now that this article had been published, everyone would be saying these things about Andre. Soon everyone would forget how kind and hardworking he was. He'd just be remembered as that guy who skipped town and kidnapped his kid.

April chose her words carefully. "He didn't seem like the type," she said. "he was a nice guy. Always wanted to make sure I got to my car safely when I left each night."

Gram shook her head. "It's the seemingly nice ones who are the worst," she said, "Because you let your guard down around them. Think of all the serial killers whose neighbors say, 'he seemed like such a nice guy.' You think if they *didn't* seem so nice they'd cause as much destruction as they do? No, because people would be wary of them. Yep, it's always the nice ones who hurt the most people."

April tried to think of something to say that wouldn't give away her investment in the topic but came up with nothing.

"Are you okay, hon?"

Gram's words drew April out of her stupor. "Huh?"

"You're just staring off into space. Your cereal's getting soggy."

"I'm fine," April said. "Just tired, I guess." She rubbed her eyes. They burned from lack of sleep.

"I know I said I'm happy you found someone, dear," Gram said. "But you really should get more rest. You're getting bags under your eyes. You're too young for that."

April nodded. "You're right, Gram. In fact, I think I'm going to go take a nap before I get ready for work." As good as a nap sounded, she was actually going to go and try to finish *The Last Adventure of Braddy Evers*.

Gram smiled, totally oblivious. "That's a great idea, dear."

~~~

April drove past Andre's apartment again on her way to work. She thought there might be a cop car in the parking lot, some evidence that the police were looking for Rico, but there was nothing, no sign that anything out of the ordinary was going on in the upstairs corner apartment. April sighed and drove to the library.

As she entered the Werner Room, she noticed that Randall and Rex were not sitting alone. Braddy sat on the chair next to him. He was reading a book (not *The First Adventure of Braddy Evers*, though his copy rested on the table next to him). With his head bent downward, he looked like a child.

April met Randall's eye, and he gave her a look that said he'd explain later. She nodded to him and walked into her office.

She'd been there for no more than ten minutes—time she spent poring over her copy of *The First Adventure of Braddy Evers,* the spine of which was quickly losing its shape—when her office door flew open.

April's heart pounded. She may have expected Thaddeus, or the cops demanding to know Rico's whereabouts. Instead, it was Rico's mom.

Her appearance had deteriorated since the previous morning. Her hair was matted, the part uneven so that a long tangle fell unattractively over her eyes. Her forehead and cheeks were shiny with sebum. She wore the same clothes she'd had on the previous day.

"Ms. Beauchamp," April said. "Can I help you with something?" It was all that she could think to say. Behind her, April could see Becky jogging up the stairs, a worried look on her face. Randall and Rex were coming towards her, too, obviously drawn by the commotion.

She lifted a single shaking finger and pointed it at April. "What are you playing at?" she said.

April's heart began to beat. Was it possible that she knew about Rico? about Andre? About everything? "W-what do you mean?"

Becky appeared in the doorway behind her. She seemed reticent to get any closer to Mrs. Beauchamp. Janet walked up and stood next to her, a concerned look on her face. Becky spoke to Janet. "She came in, yelling, asking where April was. I tried to calm her down, but she pushed past me and..." her voice grew quiet, as though she didn't want anyone to hear what she was going to say next, "she said she'd kick my ass if I tried to stop her."

"What do we do?" Janet said, her voice cracking, higher than usual. "Without a guard..."

Mrs. Beauchamp began speaking, drowning out their words. "You think I didn't see you?" she said. "I spent all day and night by that window, waiting for him to come walking up the street..." she sounded unhinged. Her words made sense, but only barely.

"See me?" April said. "Mrs. Beauchamp, I don't know what you're talking about."

She looked helplessly at Janet and Becky over the mad woman's shoulder. They stared back at her just as helplessly.

Mrs. Beauchamp laughed. It was the unrestrained guffaw of a drunkard, but she didn't smell like liquor, only body odor and cigarette smoke. "You drove past the apartment. *Twice.* I only noticed yesterday because you slowed down, then I saw the same car here in the parking lot. I told myself that you must have to drive past on the way to work. But then when you drove past again today, I decided to look up your address." She looked triumphant. "It's an extra fifteen-minute drive for you to go that way."

As she spoke, she slowly approached April. Getting closer, walking around the desk until April was pressed against one of the bookshelves on the back wall of the office.

"I-I..." she stuttered, trying to come up with a reasonable excuse for driving past Andre's apartment. It was hardly damning evidence, but as the woman drew closer, it felt like undeniable proof of her guilt.

"Where is my son!" the woman yelled, her face now less than a foot from April's. April jumped at the sudden sharpness of the words.

April was about to tell her everything, about Andre's death and how they'd covered it up, about leading Rico into the storybook world, about losing him. She'd tell her and then beg for forgiveness.

The words formed on her lips, but a dark hand appeared on Mrs. Beauchamp's shoulder. The touch seemed to shake her anger. She turned around to find Randall.

"Ma'am," Randall said. "I know you're scared and hurting, but this won't help find your son. Is this really what you want to be doing?"

She gazed into his eyes, and after a few tense seconds her face crumpled. "No." Her voice sounded like a child's.

"I know," Randall said, his deep baritone voice low and soothing. "Why don't you come out here and tell me everything, and we'll see if we can't do something about all this."

Mrs. Beauchamp deflated like a blow-up pool toy that's had the air let out of it. She looked less angry and more stunned. She allowed him to lead her out to one of the chairs in the sitting area. He asked the gawking library patrons to leave the room, and they did.

No sooner had Randall cleared her office than Janet swooped down on her.

"Are you okay? I though she was going to strangle you. We should have done something. I'm sorry."

"It's okay," April said.

"Damn it," Janet said. "We need a night guard. I don't get paid enough for this. What if she had a knife or a gun?"

Becky seemed less concerned with April's safety. She looked at April strangely. "Is it true? Did you really drive past Andre's place?"

April thought for a moment. What if Rico's mom brought this up to the police, and they started looking into her? Into the library? More than that, though, she was tired of lying. She decided to stick to the truth as closely as possible.

"I haven't been handling Andre's disappearance well," She admitted. "I mean, I was one of the last people to see him, and now he's gone. I don't know why I drove by. I thought maybe I'd see something that no one else did, and then I would be able to stop worrying about him. It was stupid. I barely knew Andre. It shouldn't affect me this much."

"Oh," Becky said, her eyes tearing up. "And all this time I thought you didn't care! I'm so sorry that I haven't been talking to you..." she threw her arms around April's shoulders. April returned the embrace awkwardly. "We'll do whatever we can to help her find Rico, and to help find Andre. I'll talk to her."

Before April could say anything else, Becky had left the room and went to go sit next to Randall and Mrs. Beauchamp. The woman was crying. Becky put her arm around her.

Janet looked down at April as though she was insane. "You should call the cops. She was about to attack you."

April shook her head. The last thing she needed was the police breathing down her neck. "She's worried about her kid, Janet. You'd do the same thing."

Janet stared out at Randall and Becky. Becky was leading Mrs. Beauchamp towards the stairs. "We were really lucky that he was here. Who would have thought crazy Randall would be able to talk someone down like that?"

April nodded. She'd forgotten that Randall was supposed to be crazy. It was hard to believe he was the same person that Becky, Janet, and Andre told her stories about when she first started.

"I think he knows what it's like to be in a bad place," April said.

Randall, seeing her watching him, waved. He seemed to be assessing her, to see if she was okay. She shrugged, hoping he would see that she was fine. Or at least as fine as it was possible to be. She must have been convincing, because he and Rex walked back down to the second floor.

Janet sighed. "I'd better get back to the desk."

Towards close, Braddy, who had been reading in a secluded corner of the Werner Room, came up and spoke to April. He was less snarky than usual, more pensive.

"So you didn't spend the day with Raoul," April asked, numbly.

Braddy shook his head. "He doesn't talk much. I'd rather be here with you all. At least there's something to read. All of his books were in a language I didn't recognize." He paused. "That was the boy's mother?"

April nodded, looking up from her copy of *The First Adventure of Braddy Evers*. She'd finished it an hour or so after going out onto the reference desk and was now rereading parts that she'd marked with sticky notes.

"She seems really upset," Braddy said.

"Yeah," April said. She waited for him to say something else, but he just returned to his chair and began reading again.

She picked up her copy of *The First Adventure of Braddy Evers* and swore under her breath as a thin section of pages fell out of the binding. She stared down at the tattered book. She got an idea.

She moved into her office and pulled out the Werner copy of *The First Adventures of Braddy Evers*, a box of binder clips, and a pair of scissors. She had work to do before nine.

~~~

They gathered around one of the study tables. April held up a handful of book pages, each section held together with a binder clip and labeled with a sticky note that noted what happened in each chapter.

"What're those?" Randall asked.

"My copy of *Braddy Evers*," she said. "I've cut it up into sections based on scenes. We can carry them through the veil and use them as references."

"You destroyed it," Randall said, wrinkling his nose in disapproval.

"Calm down," April said. "The spine was already split. It would have been weeded from the collection anyway."

She lifted the first edition copy. Sticky notes marked several spots throughout the text. "Each sticky note corresponds to a section of the book."

"Okay," Dorian said. "Why?"

"We can't tell how much time has passed in the book since yesterday, right? We've been moving from scene to scene, trying to catch up. It's not working. We need to be able to scan through the book faster."

"And how are we going to do that?"

"We're going to split up," she said. She fanned out the cut-up leaves. "The three of us—Dorian, Randall, and me—each get a section. One of us goes in, Barty closes the gate behind us, and we have fifteen minutes in library time to assess the area. Once the fifteen minutes is up, Barty opens the gate and we come back through, then on to the next one, and the next one, until we find him."

"That's an interesting plan," Dorian said, "But I don't think we should split up. Think of all the times we've had to come to each other's rescue."

Randall nodded. "And I don't know how I feel about having the gate closed behind us. What if those creepy UNC things find one of us? What if one of us gets trapped?"

April nodded. "It's risky. I wouldn't ask if I didn't believe it's the best way to find Rico. We've been playing too close to the chest. We need to take some risks." She paused. "So... will you do it?"

There was a long, pregnant pause. Then Randall nodded. "I will."

Braddy stepped forward. "I will, too."

April looked down at the groundling with a look of surprise on her face. "I thought you wanted to stay here where it was warm and safe?"

The groundling scuffed the floor with the toe of his shoe. "Seeing the boy's mother... Well, we should get him home."

April knelt in front of the groundling. "Thank you, Braddy. But you can't go in. It's too dangerous, for you *and* for Rico. If you go through and the UNCs come after you, what then? You can help best by staying here and helping Barty."

The groundling looked disappointed, but he nodded. April turned towards Dorian. "And you?"

"Of course I'm in. It's you and Randall that I'm worried about."

April nodded. "Okay. There are eighteen sections that we haven't entered. If we take them chapter by chapter, then the three of us should be able to cycle through in four rounds." She looked at Barty. "That's one hour of library time per round."

"Hold up," Randall said. "There's only one timepiece. How will Dorian and I know when we need to be back at the gate?"

April nodded. "You'll need to stay in sight distance of the gate. With the way I've divided the sections, it shouldn't be a problem."

"Actually," Barty said. "If you have more watches lying around, I think I can whip something up. It won't be as reliable as Mae's timepiece but it's better than nothing. You'll just have to sync up each time you come back into the library."

April dug through the lost and found, coming up with two watches. One was an old analog watch, the other was pink with a unicorn design on the watch's face. Barty interlaced his fingers and extended his arms until his knuckles cracked. Then he wiggled his fingers over the watches and gestured at the grandfather clock. When he was done, he held out the watches to Randall and Dorian. "That should do the trick."

Randall reached for the analog watch. "My wrist is bigger," he said.

Dorian took the unicorn watch. "I think it's rather fetching," he said.

"Ok, pretty boy." Randall snorted.

Finally ready, they stood at the gate. "The next scene after the baobhan sith was their stop at the fairy city," April said. "Is it possible they're still there? It seems like the timeline was moving faster than that."

Dorian shrugged. "It's hard to say," he said. "They'd just left Groundsville when we got there, and a whole day had passed in library time. Probably better not to chance it. I think I'd rather find them in the fairy city, anyway."

April nodded. "Okay. I'll start there." She took the corresponding stack of pages and set it aside for herself. She grabbed the next one and held it out to Randall. "After that, you'll go into the scene where the pixies attack them."

She winced. What if Randall got hurt? "Maybe I should take that one," she said. "You take the one with the fairies."

Randall shook his head and pulled the papers from her hands. "Not a chance."

She could tell there was no use arguing with him, so she turned to Dorian. "You get the scene where Braddy meets Besudel." In the book, Besudel was a pixie who'd been trapped in an underground lake by her father after she fell in love with someone he didn't approve of. Years in the dark waters turned her into a terrible monster.

Dorian nodded. "Should be easy enough."

"We need to survey the scene first. If it looks dangerous, turn back. Barty, give them a minute before you close the gate and move on to the next one, okay?"

Barty nodded. "You got it."

"The most important thing is to have the gate open fifteen minutes after the person first goes through it."

"I'll help," Braddy added.

April looked around. "Are we ready?" she said. They all nodded.

"Okay." She checked to make sure she had the correct section of *The First Adventure of Braddy Evers*. When she was ready, she said, "Open the gate."

Braddy opened the book to the first sticky note. As the gate opened, she turned back to Dorian and Randall. "Make sure you reset your watches each time you get back to the library."

They nodded, but she wasn't convinced. "Maybe I should take one of Barty's watches," she said. "If either of you got hurt..."

Dorian smirked. "We're not children, April. We'll remember to reset the watches."

"I'll remind them," Braddy chirped.

"We'd be just as upset if something happened to you," Randall said. She nodded.

The gate was open. She took a breath and stepped through.

She was in a glistening city. Tall, thin, almost-human forms floated past her, each hovering a few feet above the ground. A few of them turned to look down at her—she must still be in groundling form.

She gave a thumbs-up to the others. Barty returned the signal and Braddy closed the book. The gate closed. For a second she panicked. What if the gate didn't open on the same spot? How would she get back? She pushed the thought away. She would deal with that when and if it happened. She couldn't afford to focus on anything other than her mission: figure out if the Nisser's party had already passed through the fairy city.

She walked around. Some of the fairies glanced down at her with raised eyebrows, and a few whispered to each other, but none of them had that empty UNC dullness in their eyes.

"Excuse me," she said to a passing male fairy, but he floated by, the press of his lips the only indication that he'd heard her at all.

April approached several more fairies before one, a woman, spoke to her companion. "It speaks to us," she said. April understood the words, though she could tell that they weren't English. The sounds were too soft and elegant, like a sibilant version of tinkling bells.

"Then we should speak back," the male fairy said. "It may be entertaining."

The woman looked down at April. "Yes, small one?"

"Hello," April said. "I'm looking for my friends who rode this way. A group of a dozen Nisser, a magician, and a groundling like myself."

The female fairy nodded. "I remember them coming through. It was quite the spectacle," she didn't bother to hide her laughter. "Can you imagine so many Nisser here?"

"So they've already been here," April said impatiently.

The male spoke in the sibilant language. "Not very intelligent, this one."

"Don't be unkind," the woman said in the same language. "The queen made a pact with the Nisser prince. If she is a friend of his party, we do not want to offend her." She spoke to April in English, speaking very simply. "As I said, they were here."

"But they've already left?"

"Yes. You've missed them by about, oh, a week."

"*A week*?" April thought about Rico traveling in the cold and the rain for so long, unsure whether he'd ever get home.

The male fairy cleared his throat, and the female said, "We must be leaving. Farewell, small one."

They floated off. April checked her watch. A little less than a minute left in the library. She walked back over to the gate and waited in front of it, watching the graceful peace of the town, wishing she could stay within its borders forever. Then the gate started to open. She gave the city one last longing look and then stepped through the veil.

"Everything going smoothly?" April asked once she was back in the library. Braddy closed the book as soon as both of her feet were on the hardwood floor.

"Yeah. Randall and Dorian went in just fine. Now we're just waiting for things to come back around." Barty paused. "What did you find out?"

"I spoke to a fairy on the other side. She said that it's been a week since Rico and the dwarves moved through."

"Really?" Barty said. "The story is moving faster than we thought. Minutes here could mean days there."

"We have to find him before the story ends," April said. "How fast can you go?"

Barty scrunched his face up, doing math. "We can probably get it down to five minutes, maybe four, for each entry and exit."

April nodded. "Five at the most, okay?"

Braddy looked up at her. "What happens to the boy if we don't get to him in time?"

"We're not sure, but, as hard as it is to find him now, it will be even harder then." She paused. She wasn't sure if Braddy had finished the book or not, and didn't want to tell Braddy that his story ended with him setting off on years' worth of adventures—adventures with only a paragraph of text to pinpoint them. It would be almost impossible to find Rico if they didn't get to him before then.

The gate opened again. The other side was dark and barely visible. She grabbed the next section of the book. It was the section where Braddy reunites with the Nisser.

She stepped through, nearly slipping as her foot stepped onto something curved. She reached up to steady herself and her fingers curled around a branch. She was *in* a tree. The gate had materialized in the hollow trunk, a nest for raccoons or owls. Her heart pounded as she looked down at the ground.

"Rico? Labhras?" She called. "It's April."

There was no reply but the sound of the wind through the trees. This was stupid. Why was she wasting her time here when she knew in her heart that Rico was already weeks down the road?

She heard the gate start to close behind her and she slipped back through.

"Is something wrong?" Barty asked, surprised to see her so soon.

"Change of plans," she said. "We focus our attention at the last half of the book."

Barty looked confused. "Okay. Do you want to go into the next scene now, or do you want to talk to Dorian and Randall?"

Damn it. She should touch base with the others, but each minute here could be a hours or more there... but then they couldn't afford any mistakes because she was playing telephone.

"No. We'll regroup, first."

"Ok." Barty looked relieved. "It's nine minutes until Randall is set to come through..."

Nine minutes. How much time did that represent for Rico?

She used the time to reorganize the remaining book sections. She pushed half of them to the side and told Braddy which section in the book he needed to open to next.

"Thanks for helping," she said to him. "Especially since we kidnapped you and all."

"Don't mention it."

Randall came back through the gate. His eyes widened hopefully when he saw April. "You found him?"

April shook her head and told him what she'd learned in the fairy city, and explained her new plan. "If time is really moving that much faster," she said, "I think it's best that we focus our attention on the second half of the book."

Randall nodded. "You're right."

By the time she'd finished explaining the revised plan to Randall, the gate to Dorian's section was open. There was nothing but darkness there, and the occasional sound of water lapping against stone.

April watched the clock tick down. The fifteen-minute mark passed. "He should be back by now."

"Maybe his watch is running slow," Barty replied, though he sounded nervous.

April nodded, hoping that that was it. They waited another minute, each passing tick of the clock reducing her hope that Dorian would appear on his own. She approached the gate, trying to make out shapes in the murky darkness, but she couldn't. At about waist-height, there was movement. She focused on it and realized that there was waist-high water on the other side. The gate had opened in the underground lake. Tiny rivulets of swampy liquid ran down around the edges of the veil.

A scream emitted somewhere in the cave and echoed off the cave walls, distorted by the water.

"He's in trouble," April said. "I'm going in."

Before they could stop her, she plunged through the gate. The water was murky and cold, though not frigid.

"Where is it?" A voice emerged from the darkness. It sounded slimy and breathy and desperate, the voice of a thing that's lived in shadow for longer than it can remember.

There was splashing, and small waves of water lapped against her knees.

Her eyes slowly adjusted to the darkness. She was in a giant, roughly dome-shaped cavern half-filled with water. The water level rose and fell rhythmically by about a foot, and as it receded she saw the tops of several dark outlets where the water must be moving in and out. An island of rock rose from the water ten feet away. Dorian sat at the edge of the rock, staring at the water in consternation.

A head broke the surface, long, dark lanks of hair clung to its scalp, the ends floating in the water like seaweed. Only the creature's eyes and nose were above the water. It stared up at Dorian like a hungry shark.

She heard a splash near the veil. The form that floated next to her was so small it could only be Braddy.

"What are you doing here?" she hissed. "Go back!"

"I want to help," he whispered. "After I read the book, I did some research on Besudel. I think I know how to beat her." Before she could stop him, he called out. "Over here!"

"What is this?" Besudel said. She had raised up slightly so that her mouth was above the water, but only barely. When she spoke, streams of water entered her mouth so that her words came out as a gurgle. "More meat? Lucky day! I won't let you slip away like my last meal."

April heard Braddy swallow, but when he spoke again his voice was sure. "Yes, I have sought you out. You recently let one of your captives escape. He's been bragging about how easy it was to evade the great and terrible Besudel. I couldn't believe a creature could be so dim-witted and slow, so I came to see for myself."

Besudel's outraged roar was choked as she disappeared under the water. Her back formed a fin-like protrusion on the lake's surface as she swam in Braddy's direction. Braddy waved one shaking hand at April. "Get Dorian," he hissed, and April hesitated only a moment before moving towards the stone island where Dorian was perched.

Behind her, Besudel broke the surface a few feet in front of Braddy. The groundling was shaking, but he held his ground.

For a moment, April thought Besudel was going to attack. Instead, she said in a petulant voice, "Lies! He escaped unfairly."

"That's not what he said," Braddy said skeptically.

Besudel hissed angrily. "Lies!"

"Okay, okay," Braddy said in a reasonable tone. "Would you like to redeem yourself?"

"Yes, yes!" Besudel crowed. "I will beat you, and then I will eat you!"

"Hold on," Braddy said. "I want to make this fair." he said. "I heard that you are a talented singer. Perhaps a singing contest?"

"Intriguing," Besudel gurgled. "It is true that I possessed the most beautiful singing voice in all of the pixie kingdom. I was the envy of my father's court. You have no hope of winning against me." She paused. "But who will judge this contest?"

"Well, perhaps the person on that ledge, there," Braddy said. "And if I win, you must let both him and I leave. Deal?"

"Person?" Besudel sounded genuinely confused. "You mean the meat. And when I win, I eat BOTH of you!"

"Yes, quite," Braddy said, obviously flustered. He waved behind his back at April and pointed in Dorian's direction. The message was clear: get Dorian, so that they could get out of there before Besudel got a chance to make good on her promise.

April didn't need to be told twice. She moved towards the island. One side was lifted a few feet above the water, but the other was a small beach that she could walk on. The water slowed her steps, and she dared not go faster lest she make noise and alert Besudel to her presence.

"Well, go on," Besudel said impatiently. "Sing!"

"Uh, ladies first," Braddy insisted, and April realized that he was trying to give her more time.

"Chivalry will get you nowhere down here," Besudel laughed cruelly, but then she cleared her throat, and raised herself up slightly so that her mouth was above the water, then she began to sing.

The sound that echoed around the cavern was less like speech than it was like singing bowls, or the deepest tones of a pipe organ. There were no words. It was undoubtedly beautiful, but dark and haunting.

The last tone faded, and Besudel plunged back down so that her mouth was partially in the water. She laughed into the water. "I've still got it!" she crowed. "You are doomed, meat-bag. You cannot possibly hope to beat me. Maybe I should just eat you now..."

April paused on on the stone embankment. She should help Braddy... or should she keep going after Dorian? She froze, unable to decide.

"No!" Braddy said. He motioned for her to keep going. "I at least deserve a chance. Unless you're a cheater after all..."

"I am not a cheat!" Besudel yelled, enraged. "I will win fair and square! Sing, so I may sooner feel your flesh beneath my teeth."

"Fine," Braddy said, a tremor in his voice. "Okay. What to sing, what to sing..."

"Hurry up!"

"Song choice is important, you know," Braddy said. "Ah, okay, I've got it..."

April was on the beach now, walking in only an inch or so of water. The sound of water dripping from her clothes onto the beach seemed impossibly loud, but Besudel didn't seem to notice. She started to move more quickly but collided with something warm. In the dim light she made out Dorian's angelic, worried features.

"You're here. How did you know I needed help?" he said, he sounded frightened. He squeezed her hand.

"How many times have you saved me?" she grasped his hand. "Let's go."

Braddy began to sing, in a warbling, serviceable voice that didn't come close to matching Besudel's:

"Nyk, Nyk,
Needle in the water,
The Virgin Mary threw steel in the water,
You are sinking, I float."

The groundling stepped backwards. "It didn't work... April!"

"What is this? Who are you talking to?" The change in Besudel's tone drew April's attention. She was no longer talking to Braddy, but instead stood up, with her chest and arms now above the water. She looked directly at them. "Trickery!" Besudel roared.

"No, no no—we need to finish our contest! I need to sing the next verse. It's in Scandinavian..." Braddy said, but Besudel was already splashing towards April and Dorian. They moved down into the water, moving as fast as possible towards the gate. Besudel disappeared under the water's surface. There was no way they'd be able to outswim her.

"Go!" Dorian said. "I'll distract it, I'll—"

But it was too late for that. Besudel emerged from the depths only feet in front of them. She smiled as her head broke the surface, revealing blackened, rotting nubs that used to be teeth.

In the low glint from the gate, they saw a rock sail towards Besudel, smacking her wetly in the side of the head and throwing her off balance. They looked towards the source of the rock throwing and saw Braddy. She looked completely shocked at his own action.

Besudel shrieked in pain and anger. "How dare you!" She sank down into the water until only the top of her head was visible, and began streaking towards Braddy like a shark.

"Braddy!" April yelled.

"Go!" the groundling yelled at them before running further up onto the beach.

"He's going the wrong way," April said. "He won't be able to get back to the gate..."

"He's distracting Besudel so that we can get out," Dorian said. "Come on. Let's not make him act in vain." He tugged her away.

She allowed herself to be pushed through the veil; water gushed around her as she crossed it, but the flow was staunched again after Dorian was through.

"Braddy?" Barty said.

She shook her head, unable to say the words.

They heard Besudel swimming directly towards the open gate.

"Close it!" Dorian said.

After only the slightest hesitation, Barty closed the book. The gate began to close. When it was half-closed, Besudel's arms pierced the veil, grasping at the air. April was sure her arm would be severed by the edges of the stained-glass, but she pulled it back at the last moment, scraping her skin raw on the jagged edge. The last thing April heard from the other side was a hiss of pain and anger.

"We just left him over there." Barty said.

"We'll go back for him," Dorian said. "Once we figure out a plan..."

"I appreciate your concern," Braddy's voice came from the air near the middle window, "But I am very much all right." The air distorted and then parted, revealing Braddy. It was like he had been wrapped in a blanket painted to look exactly like the library behind him. He pulled the fabric off, and it almost disappeared again, but became more apparent when it moved, like smudged paint.

"You're alive!" April said. "What was all that back there? I thought you said you knew how to beat Besudel?"

Braddy looked a little sheepish. "I thought I did. After I finished the book, I did some research. It turns out the author based Besudel on a water monster called the Noekken. The words I said are supposed to confuse the Noekken to let you escape. In theory."

"Some theory," Randall said. "You almost died in there!"

"Well, some good came out of it." Braddy held up the fabric. "The cape of vanishing, just like in the book. I found it on the stone beach—slipped on it, actually. I'm a good sneak-thief after all, eh?"

Randall stared at the coat, his eyes wide. "That isn't... that's not... *the* coat, is it?"

"It made him invisible," Dorian said. "I'd say it is."

"But how is that possible? Rico should have found it and taken it."

He was right. In the book, the fairy queen had given the cape to Braddy as a gift, and he'd had it all the way through the book until he entered the stollenwurm's lair. It was cited as the reason he was able to find the stollenwurm's key. She looked at Dorian. "What does this mean?"

"It means we need to find Rico," he said gravely. "This has unsettling implications."

"Like?" April asked.

"If this can change, anything else in the storyline can change."

"What does that mean?" Randall asked.

April answered. "It's possible that he could fail at the things Braddy succeeded at in the book. Or worse."

"Hmm," Randall said. "We'd better go, then."

"You're right," Dorian said. "But why are we all here at the same time, anyway? Shouldn't you both be in your next scenes?"

They explained to him that the story was moving faster than they'd expected, and their plan to jump ahead in the book.

Dorian nodded. "We can't afford to waste time. But where do we start?" He asked. "The fairy woman said it's been a week... how much time has passed while we've been dealing with Besudel? We don't have enough information to guess accurately."

April reached down and lifted one of the book sections. It was the section where Braddy first enters the lair of the stollenwurm. April had been hopeful when she read the word "wurm," but Randall had informed her a stollenwurm was basically the same thing as a dragon, only scarier.

"Are you sure?" Dorian asked. "That may be the most dangerous section in the book."

April shook her head. "I have a feeling that this is it. I can't explain it."

Dorian nodded. "Mae would get intuitions, too."

"Were they right?" April asked.

"Not always," Dorian said. "But they were right more often than they were wrong."

"I trust you," Randall said. "Let's do it. If he's not there, then we either work our way backwards or forwards depending on what the scene looks like."

April nodded, though she knew in her gut that he'd be there. How did she know this, and why hadn't the instinct kicked in earlier? How much trouble could have been avoided if she could have looked at the book and known where Rico was two nights ago?

But she didn't have time to think about that. She needed her full concentration on the task at hand. She looked up at Dorian and Randall. "Together?"

They nodded. "Together," Dorian said.

"What about me?" Braddy asked.

"Is there a possibility of Braddy attracting UNCs?" April asked.

Randall opened a paperback copy of *The First Adventure of Braddy Evers* to the map on the inside cover. He pointed at a small triangle. "The area seems pretty isolated. Minimal risk."

Dorian spoke. "It's now or never for making the switch," he said. "Braddy needs to be their regardless."

April nodded. She spoke to Braddy. "Stay out of sight until it's time."

Braddy nodded.

"There's one other thing," Randall said. "In the book, Braddy uses the cape to hide from the stollenwurm. If Braddy has the coat here, that means Rico doesn't."

April nodded. "We need to reach him before he faces the stollenwurm."

Barty opened *The First Adventure of Braddy Evers*. The gate opened to darkness.

"Where's it opening at?" Randall asked.

Dorian spoke grimly. "Well, the gate likes doors. There's one large door in the side of the mountain. It doesn't look like it's opening up onto the outward-facing side, so..."

"Straight into the stollenwurm's lair."

"Yep."

"Great."

The darkness they stepped into was different than the darkness of Besudel's underground lake. The air was dry enough to make April crave a glass of ice water. The smell of smoke and something rancid that April hoped wasn't rotting flesh tinged the air.

"Where are we?"

"In the tunnel leading into the mountain. The walls are smooth..." there was a rubbing sound of Dorian trailing his hand along the stone wall.

"Well, let's follow it," April said. "Keep your eyes open."

They followed the path, clasping hands and trailing their fingers along the stone to make sure they didn't veer off into the wrong direction. Rex, who seemed comfortable following his nose, led the way. He growled every so often.

They walked so far that April wondered if they were going the wrong way, though there hadn't been any forks in the tunnel. Still, she couldn't help but feel that something was wrong, something atmospheric.

Then she realized what it was. The tunnel was filled with the push and pull of air as though from a temperamental old furnace—it was like being inside a giant iron lung. There was even the singe that air had when it was blown past hot metal. But it wasn't a furnace. It was breath, the source of the rancid, old-meat stink. What kind of creature was so large that it pushed air through a tunnel this size just by breathing?

Dorian squeezed her hand. He'd noticed, too.

"At least we know we're going in the right direction," she whispered.

"Define 'right direction,'" Randall muttered. No one answered him.

"Still want to see a stollenwurm?" Dorian asked.

"Hush."

They continued to walk towards the breathing... or was it snoring? The sound grew louder, and the air flow became strong enough that tendrils of hair pulled free from her bun and billowed around her face.

There was something else, a new noise separate from the rhythmic breathing. She stopped walking.

"What is it?" Dorian asked, tension in his voice.

"Shh," she said, and listened. The others listened with her. She was sure that they, too, were holding their breath...

There it was, in the pause between the stollenwurm's inhale and exhale. A sniffle, the sucking in of shaking breath.

April let go of Dorian's hand and strode towards the sound as quickly as the darkness allowed, ignoring the others' concerned whispers. She focused on the whimpering until it was only a few feet away.

"Hello?" she said in the darkness.

The whimpering intensified. "Wh-who's there? Don't come any closer—I'm armed!" The sound of metal scraping against stone echoed through the tunnel. He must have picked up a sword.

"Rico!" she said. The tension that had been building in her body since the moment Rico ran away from her at the party partially released, though not all the way. She knew she still had to get him out of there. This game hadn't been won, not yet.

There was a surprised pause in the whimpering. "How do you know that name?"

"It's me, April," she said. "I've been looking for you. Are you all right?" She reached out towards him and her hand brushed his hair, inches longer than it was the last time she'd seen him.

He grabbed her hand, gripping it as though he didn't believe she was real, and if he didn't have a hold of her she might disappear back into the darkness. "Is it really you?"

"Yes. I'm sorry we didn't come sooner. We were searching for so long..." she trailed off, afraid that she might start crying. She didn't want to scare him further.

"I made a mistake in Besudel's lair," he said. "I got so scared that I climbed out early, and the cape of vanishing fell off. I tried to go back, but it was too late." His voice cracked. "If I try to fight the stollenwurm, he'll see me!"

"Shh," April said. "Shh. You don't have to. I promise, you're safe."

Dorian and the others slowly approached. The boy shrank back from them. "It's okay. They're my friends."

Braddy stuck out his hand and gripped Rico's. "I'm the groundling whose role you've taken," he said, almost too cheerfully. "It's nice to finally meet you."

"Braddy?" Rico said. He took the groundling's outstretched hand. "Nice to meet you, too. Sorry for taking over your life. You've been with them the whole time?"

"Long story," Dorian said. "We'll explain later. How have you managed to get through the story, anyway?"

"Well, Dad used to read this book to me before bed when I was little, so I was familiar with it. When it was time for me to say something or do something, it was like I remembered it perfectly in my head. Until now, though. All the book says is that Braddy used the cape to outsmart the stollenwurm, but..." he trailed off.

"It's okay," April said. "You don't have to go back there."

"That's right," Braddy said. "We just need to switch places."

"It's not that," Rico said. "I'm not sure I *want* to go back."

"*What?*" April couldn't believe what she was hearing.

"I know I'm crying like a stupid little kid," he said, "but all this has been awesome. It was hard at first. I was cold and alone and scared and everyone would act really weird when I tried to tell them who I was. But it got easier. Now I'm this badass sneak-thief." He paused. "And..."

April finished for him. "You're dad's not dead here."

His head rose up and down slightly in the dim light.

To April's surprise, it was Braddy who spoke. "I was sad to hear about your father's passing," he said, "But you shouldn't let that loss cloud your mind from what's left."

"Which is what?" Rico said, defiant.

"Your mother needs you. She's out of her mind with worry."

"Mom?" Rico snorted. "She's too busy talking smack about Dad. She doesn't give a crap about me."

"Young man, nothing could be further from the truth. Now, why don't you give me that sword, and we'll both go back where we belong." When Rico didn't move, he said, "Don't you think I deserve a little adventure, too?"

Rico gripped the handle of the small sword and scabbard attached to his belt. He held onto it, motionless, for several more seconds. Then he removed it and handed it to Braddy.

April looked at the groundling. "The storyline's been broken," she said. "There's no guarantee that... that things will turn out like they do in the book." She couldn't let him go without knowing for sure that he was aware of this fact.

"It's not an adventure if there's no danger, is it?" He lifted the cape up over his head. "Come over for tea some time, won't you? Once this is all over?"

"Of course," April said.

Braddy closed the cape and disappeared. The empty air where he'd stood said, "Thanks for the adventure." The patter of tiny feet receded into the darkness.

"Is he going to be okay?" Rico asked.

April nodded. She wasn't sure, but she knew there was nothing she could do about it either way. "I think so."

"Let's get back to the gate," Dorian said.

From behind them came a deep croaking sound, like the earth was wrenching itself in two, that made them all jump.

"Yeah," Randall said. "You're right."

They jogged back to the gate. Before stepping through, Rico turned to look behind him. "Goodbye," he said.

Chapter Ten

Thaddeus again sat in the seat in front of Mason's desk, his knees cramping.

Mason was talking at length about his teenaged daughter's homecoming dance, which had taken place a few weeks prior. Mason had started the conversation by asking if Thaddeus wanted kids, to which Thaddeus had replied no.

Finally, Mason changed the subject. "So, the Pagewalker. Has she accepted your offer?"

Thaddeus squirmed. "No, sir."

Mason nodded. "That is unfortunate. With training she would have been a great asset to us."

"So what do we do now?"

"Like I said before—our next step is to escalate our tactics."

"And how do we do that?" Thaddeus asked, though he knew the answer.

"What made the Jackson woman so goddamn untouchable was how she managed to isolate herself. Whatever weaknesses she had, she certainly didn't show them to us. This new Pagewalker, this girl, hasn't realized the need yet."

"What do you suggest, sir?"

Mason reached into his desk and pulled out a black folder. He opened it up. Paperclipped to one side was a picture of the Pagewalker photocopied from a student I.D. Thaddeus had reviewed the file before he first contacted her. The other pages included all the information the agency had managed to put together, including her physical description, medical history, and more.

Mason pulled out a thin stack of papers that Thaddeus hadn't seen before. It was a write-up similar to that about April, but it was instead on her grandmother. The packet included a photocopy of a membership card scraped from the systems of a gym, plus photos of the woman sitting in a café with friends.

"What is this?" Thaddeus asked.

"This," Mason said. "Is the Pagewalker's weakness."

Chapter Eleven

April didn't know what Rico told his mother, or how he'd explained the fact that his hair had grown an inch in three days. She must have been so happy to have him that she was willing to overlook these details, because she came in the next morning to let the library staff know he'd shown up. Rico wasn't with her. April hoped he was okay.

She and the others still met every weeknight to combat the ink rot, but thanks to the break-neck pace they'd been working at, there was less and less of it until they were able to go home after an hour or two.

The following Friday after Barty and Randall had left for the night, April walked over to the Werner shelves.

Dorian walked up behind her. "*One Thousand and One Nights?*" He asked. "Not that it's any of my business."

"No." she pulled *The First Adventure of Braddy Evers* off the shelf, then opened it to the beginning. "Just wanted to see if Braddy's home yet. Want to come?"

Dorian shrugged. "Why not?"

The walk down the road to Ever Home was uneventful. April rapped on Braddy's door gently. No answer. She sighed and leaned against the door.

"Are you worried about him?" Dorian asked.

"A little," she said. "Shouldn't he be back?"

"It depends. Maybe the story isn't done yet. Maybe he decided to go on more adventures rather than return here."

"I hope so."

"We'll keep trying."

April looked up at the stars, which were brighter than any she'd ever seen at home in the city. She laid down in Braddy's garden and stared up at the sky. Dorian lay down next to her. He pulled off his jacket and lay it out beneath their heads.

"Did we ruin this world?" April asked.

Dorian sighed. "I'm really not sure how to answer that. You seem to take things pretty hard. If anything can be construed as remotely your fault, you fall to pieces. No offense."

She was about to argue, then sighed. "That's fair."

"We probably knocked this world off course, but can you really say that's not how things were supposed to happen in the first place? Does this world really look ruined?"

She gazed up at the thousands of twinkling lights showing between the tops of the massive trees. She thought about how Braddy knew about the danger and chose to face it anyway. "No."

"So, there. It's not ruined. Different, maybe."

"Will it ever become like the other books again? Like, will the story reset itself?"

Dorian shook his head. "I don't think so. I believe this world will just continue on." He added sarcastically, "though every day with you is disproving something I once thought was fact."

"Existing between the lines," April said.

"Yes." He propped himself up on his elbow and looked at her. He lifted his free hand, and for a second she thought he might reach out and touch her face.

But then his open, peaceful expression darkened and he lay back down and looked up at the stars. They watched the sky for a few more minutes, then he said, "I have something I want to ask you but I'm afraid to."

"What?" She said, feeling the anxiety rise up in her chest again.

"The night Rico got lost... you said he saw one of the black books. Why did you have it open in the first place?"

She thought back. Why had she opened it? It seemed so long ago now. "I don't know," she said. "I thought that if I could save enough people from the rot it would make up for what happened to Andre."

"You weren't planning on going in, were you?" His voice was tense.

"No," she said. "Not really. I mean, the thought crossed my mind for like, a split second. I just... it's hard to explain. I guess I just thought seeing was better than leaving them forgotten beneath the floorboards. It was, like, my penance to witness what they were going throught."

Dorian said up and looked at her. "*Penance?*" he said. "You were talking to Reverend Dimmesdale, weren't you?"

She nodded. "He's a priest, right? He has to know what he's talking about."

Dorian pinched the bridge of his nose. "The whole point of *The Scarlet Letter* is to face your mistakes and not let them eat away at you. *To move on.* Taking advice about guilty consciences from Arthur Dimmesdale! You really need to read more."

He lay back down. They remained in silence for several minutes. Just when April was going to say they should head back into the library, he spoke again.

"And if you had gone into that book, where would that leave the rest of us?"

"You would have found someone else to be the Pagewalker. Someone better. Then you wouldn't have to deal with me anymore."

Dorian sat up. He looked agitated. "Is that really what you think? That I was saddled with you and am now making do?"

"Well, yeah."

"It's not true, April. You're smart, kind, And," he said, a smile on his face, "You don't let anyone push you around."

"That sounds like what you say to make someone feel better."

"It's not. How many people would have done everything you did to find Rico? How many would have put their life on hold to help their grandmother? How many would *care* about the people in the black books? Most people would say 'that's not my problem,' or, 'I can't worry about that right now.' Not you."

"But I did think those things!" She said.

"And you keep doing this anyway!"

"It's what anyone would do."

"No, they wouldn't." Dorian looked agitated. "I've been in hundreds of books and dealt with thousands of different people. The majority are self-centered and short-sighted." He sighed. "So please don't think you'd do anyone any favors by disappearing. Me least of all."

"Oh." April couldn't think of anything else to say. "I always thought you were annoyed by me."

"*What?*" He saw the look on her face then said, "Well, if I am it's because I think you need to give yourself some slack. Most of the time."

She was about to argue some more but he held up his hand. "Just... trust me."

The earnest expression on his face made her nod. They lay back down on the ground and stared up at the stars.

"I did learn one thing through all this, though," Dorian mused.

"Oh, yeah? What's that?"

"I need to assign you a reading list. Starting Monday."

April groaned.

~~~

April leaned against the wall, a cup of bitter hospital coffee cooling in her hands. Gram preferred privacy during her checkups, so April waited in the hallway. The fluorescent light made her eyes water.

An alcove across the hall was filled with children's toys and a small television played cartoons. It was empty except for a small boy playing with a set of Legos and his mother, who surreptiously watched him while she flipped thorugh a magazine. The boy looked up at April shyly. His eyes were bright blue. Except for a man walking down the hallway towards her, the place was empty.

She watched the boy a few moments longer. It wasn't until the man came and stood next to her that she recognized him. *Thaddeus.* She was suddenly wide awake.

She looked around. Should she yell for help? Run? Calling out was a bad idea—what would she say to the people who came to help her? He hadn't done anything to her. Yet. Running was an even worse action. What if he went after Gram?

She took a sip of her coffee, careful not to let the shaking of her hands show. She noted a security camera in the corner of the alcove. He wouldn't do anything to her in front of it, would he?

Well, she wasn't going to let him know he'd spooked her. "What do you want?" she asked, like he was no more than an old high school enemy.

He held up his hands to show they were empty. "Just to talk."

"Yeah, right."

He reached out towards her neck. She would have pulled away if she wasn't against the wall. He lifted the stone amulet Barty had given her. It had slipped out from beneath the collar of her blouse.

"A protection amulet? I see our would-be warlock is back in town. I imagine it's supposed to glow if I mean you harm, is it not? So either I'm telling the truth, or your friend isn't as competent as he believes."

He was right, the amulet was as dull and unattractive as ever. She wasn't convinced—Barty's charms had failed before—but what else could she do? She took another sip of coffee to keep the cup from spilling in her shaking hands.

"I hate hospitals," he said, glancing around with distaste. "You should have taken the deal I offered. Your grandmother could be on her way to a full recovery now."

"She wasn't going to do the treatment anyway. She said she didn't want to spend her last days being prodded by needles."

Thaddeus nodded. "I respect a person who can look death in the face with acceptance. Too much of the human existence is spent shying away from the inevitable rather than enjoying the miracle that is life."

She looked sideways at him. He sounded like a religious person who might invite her to a singles mixer at his church. She could tell he believed what he was saying.

"You have no idea what you've taken on. You chose the wrong side."

"I chose the side that hasn't killed a bunch of people and isn't okay with killing a bunch more. Seems like the right one to me."

He wrinkled his brow as though the accusation confused him. "Do you mean the wizards? The otherkin? They're dangerous. Humans once lived in fear of them. The life you live now, all of *this*"—he swept his arm around his head to indicate the hospital—"is only possible because of what my forefathers did."

"The victors do get to write history."

"I suppose that's true," Thaddeus said, "though now we're the evil overlords, so we didn't get to write it too much." He shrugged. "Even the Catholic church was an underdog once. Now it's one of the most powerful and corrupt institutions in the world."

"What do you want, Thaddeus?"

"I told you my superiors want to come at you with everything they have. They've decided harsher tactics are necessary."

"What are you talking about?" she asked.

He looked at her gravely. "I was able to find you here. They will, too. They know about your grandmother, and anyone and anything else you hold dear, and they will use them against you."

"Gram isn't involved in this!"

"She is, whether you like it or not."

Her pulse fluttered in the back of her throat. She turned to run down the hall towards the room where Gram was, but Thaddeus stepped in front of her, almost pinning her against the wall.

"They're not here. But if they were, what could you do? Nothing."

She stopped. He was right. "Why are you telling me this?"

He sighed. "My superiors and I have a very different outlook on our mission. They are willing to sacrifice the lives of innocents to achieve their goals."

"And you're not?"

He paused. "Casualties are... inevitable," he said, "But I believe they must be minimized. Our goal is to protect people from magic, not kill them anyway in the process." He turned to her. "They will come for you. They'll come for your grandmother, and they'll come for your friends. They will show no mercy."

"Then help us, if you care so much."

"I can't. If they knew I was talking to you..." he paused. "Just prepare yourself, though I'm not even sure you can do anything."

He turned and walked back in the direction he'd come from.

She watched him go, a sinking feeling in her chest. She was *so* screwed.

~~~

Thanks for reading!

You just finished *Spinebreaker,* book two in the Pagewalker series. Thank you so much for reading! If you liked this book, please consider leaving an honest review on Amazon. Leaving reviews is the number one way to support writers. As a new indie author, I truly appreciate it.

-H. Duke

http://www.hdukeauthor.com

More books by H. Duke

Fantasy
Jeremiah Jones Cowboy Sorcerer Series
Jeremiah Jones Cowboy Sorcerer: The Complete First Season
Season One Episode One
Season One Episode Two
Season One Episode Three
Season One Episode Four
Season One Episode Five
Season One Episode Six
Season One Episode Seven
Season One Episode Eight
A Cowboy Sorcerer Christmas (email list exclusive)
Taming the Wolf (email list exclusive)
The Pagewalker Series
Pagewalker
Spinebreaker
Wordeater
The First Adventure of Braddy Evers
Horror (written as H. H. Duke)
Things on the Shelf: Three Tales of Christmas Terror
Find an up-to-date list at *http://www.hdukeauthor.com*

About the Author

H. Duke has written over ten works of fiction, including the weird west serial *Jeremiah Jones Cowboy Sorcerer* and the Library Gate books.

These days, she can be seen travelling the United States in her travel trailer with her husband Giru and a shiny black dog named Jupiter. To see an up-to-date list of her works and find out where she'll be writing next, visit *http://www.hdukeauthor.com.*

www.ingramcontent.com/pod-product-compliance
Lightning Source LLC
Chambersburg PA
CBHW052000170626
46808CB00007B/2711